STEVE YOUNG

15
Minutes

HarperCollins*Publishers*

15 Minutes

Copyright © 2006 by Steve Young

All rights reserved. No part of this book may be used or reproduced in any manner whatsoever without written permission except in the case of brief quotations embodied in critical articles and reviews. Printed in the United States of America. For information address HarperCollins Children's Books, a division of HarperCollins Publishers, 1350 Avenue of the Americas, New York, NY 10019.

www.harpercollinschildrens.com

Library of Congress Cataloging-in-Publication Data is available.
ISBN-10: 0-06-072508-7 — ISBN-13: 978-0-06-072508-2
ISBN-10: 0-06-072509-5 (lib. bdg.)
ISBN-13: 978-0-06-072509-9 (lib. bdg.)

Typography by Amy Ryan

1 2 3 4 5 6 7 8 9 10

❖

First Edition

to kelly and casey
or
casey and kelly,
who can no longer argue
over whose name I placed first

Time is something that takes just so much . . . time. Yet if you have ever sat through the last two minutes of a football game, you begin to understand that time can take a lot more time than you could ever imagine.

1

2

3

I Finally Show Up

Casey Little here. Sorry about making you wait. I really wasn't paying attention to the time. The problem is, I never do. I'm late. I'm late all the time.

People say I got it from my grandfather Jesse. My *late* grandfather Jesse. My mother complains that I'd be late for my own funeral. I wonder if my grandfather showed up on time for his, though to tell you the truth, I wouldn't show up at all for mine.

Mom is right about me never being on time. That's why I'm just writing this now. I would've started earlier but—well, you know.

One day, about a month ago, something happened so

5

unbelievably *timely* that my entire world was turned upside down. Not that Australia was on the top and we were on the bottom, but it felt that way.

It all started very, very quietly.

4

The Big Game!
(Okay, Maybe Not That Quietly)

There was only time for one more play, and we were eighty yards from pay dirt. Our quarterback, Todd Dornan, took the ball and dropped back, looking for a receiver. As usual, I was the receiver he was looking for. Also as usual, I had two defenders covering me. I made two quick fakes and left them far behind.

I took off for the end zone and, as usual, Todd delivered the ball perfectly into my hands. Sidestepping the last defender with a chance to stop me, I was just about to score the winning touchdown when . . .

"Casey! Casey Little, you wake up this instant! You're going to be late for school!"

"I am up!" I yelled back, though not nearly as loud as Mom. To be perfectly honest, I wasn't really up. I've just developed an ability to respond to my parents without waking up. Besides, that was only her fourth wake-up yell. It usually takes a good seven yells before I roll out of bed.

How many yells does it take for you to get up?

"(Your answer here)"

Man, you're worse than me.

"Casey!"
"Casey!"
"Casey!"

Mom had become pretty shrewd about getting all seven wake-up yells in as quickly as possible. Still, I wish she would wait until I finished my dream. I've had that dream a zillion times and I don't think I ever finished it, unless that's the way it's supposed to finish. Pretty lame ending, if you ask me.

I checked my clock. It was 6:30 A.M. You'd think it was a pretty good time to get up. And it would have been if my clock hadn't broken three weeks ago, at 6:30 A.M. Today, at 8:00 A.M., I hadn't even brushed my teeth.

I started getting ready as fast as I could, but just as sure as the sun comes up (I'm sure it does, though I've never been up early enough to actually see it), I'd be late for school.

"Casey!"
"I'm up, Mom."

5

Maybe This Time

I never had time for breakfast. It wasn't my fault. Mom just felt that it had to be eaten in the morning.

"Casey," said Dad, shaking his head. "You'll never be the football player you can be if you don't start getting on the ball."

I don't think "getting on the ball" had anything to do with it. Lack of any skill was more my problem. When you were a high school All-State football player, like Dad was, I think it's hard to understand that becoming a great player isn't all that easy. It's not that he wasn't supportive. Every day after school Dad would have a catch with me. Actually, with me, it wasn't as much of a catch as a miss. He'd never said it, but I'm sure he was disappointed I wasn't the player he had been.

"Look at the time," said Mom, pretty much the same

thing she said every morning.

"What?" I asked. "Am I early?"

Funny how she didn't find that . . . funny.

I grabbed my backpack, ran out the door, and jumped on my bike.

"Ow!"

I have got to remember to buy a seat.

My house was only twelve blocks away from school, and if I rode that bike as fast as I could, there would actually be a chance that I could get there on . . .

Ri-i-i-i-ing!

. . . time.

Man, that school bell really carries. And there I was, pedaling as fast as I could, a good four blocks away. Actually, it wasn't so bad. I'm normally seven or eight blocks away when the bell rings. Unfortunately, they don't give prizes for being not-as-late-as-you-normally-are . . . not anymore. They felt the prizes were counterproductive. Besides, I had already retired the trophy.

6

classy Entrance

I headed for my homeroom. Ms. Loozer's homeroom. I know. It's pretty sad. Even though she pronounced it "Low-ser." Everyone else in school pronounced it just like you would: "Loser." It didn't help that most of us in Loozer's class were—how should I put it?—losers. It wasn't that we were dumb. At least, not all of us. But coincidentally, I think, we were all rather inept at something. Maybe a lot of things.

Howie "See You Next Fall" Dansky couldn't put one foot in front of the other without tripping.

Geri "Nervous" Pervis was the smartest girl in school, but she was one of those people who worried about everything, so much so that when she worried, she worried that she wasn't worrying enough.

Mel "Say It, Don't Spray It" Kardos couldn't speak two words without spitting on anyone within a radius of ten feet.

Joy "Stick" Short was 110 pounds, an ideal weight for many girls. Unfortunately, she was also the perfect height for a boy—six foot two.

Jack "Can You Hear Me Now?" Miller had ears an African elephant would die for.

And there were more. Somehow we all found our way into Ms. Loozer's class. The more I think about it, the more I believe that we didn't end up in the same class by accident.

I walked into class, trying to act nonchalant, hoping Ms. Loozer wouldn't notice that I was late. And it almost worked except—

"Ms. Loozer, look what time it is."

Darn, my big, big mouth.

"Well, Mr. Little," said Ms. Loozer. "It's so nice of you to join us."

Oh, if she only meant it.

"After class, would you like to grace Principal Gordon with your presence?"

Was she giving me a choice? Could I refuse to go? After all, she did ask it in the form of a question.

"No, I was not asking a question, and no, you cannot refuse."

Geez Louise. Ms. Loozer could read my mind.

"I cannot read your mind, Mr. Little. You've been speaking out loud."

Darn.

"And congratulations are in order, Mr. Little," announced Ms. Loozer.

Finally. Good news. Or would this be one of those set-me-up-then-mow-me-down insults?

"You have set an all-time class record."

Wow. That's got to be good.

"You didn't get one answer right on yesterday's history test."

Maybe not that good.

"And that's on a true-or-false test."

There goes the "at least you've got a 50 percent chance you'll get it right" theory.

"You even spelled your name wrong."

Still, with my new record as a distraction, I could pretty much twist Ms. Loozer around my little finger.

wrong!

A year of detention if I'm late again?

Ms. Loozer has got to get a sense of humor.

"Man, you have got to get a watch," said my best bud, Nina Pinsky.

We have known each other forever. She is one of those tomboy types who can skateboard better than most boys can walk. The kind who tucks her long blond hair under her Yankees baseball cap and wears clothes that she thinks make her look tough. But—and you gotta swear not to tell her, no matter how hard she tries to hide it—she is about the best-looking thirteen-year-old tomboy you'd ever want to see. It's not like I could look at her in *that way*. I mean, she's my best friend. You just don't look at best friends in *that way*. You can, but then you better forget about the friendship. Or at least that's what my dad says.

"Casey! Ms. Loozer is serious," Nina said. "This stuff goes on your permanent record. You could even end up failing. Do you know what it'll be like to be held back while everyone you know gets promoted?"

"Yeah. I'll finally be taller than some kids."

"Real funny."

But I'm pretty sure she didn't mean it.

"Casey. You can joke all you want, but when I'm in college and you're still in seventh grade, don't expect me to hang out with you in the principal's office. I'll be too busy with my college boyfriends who are always on time."

"Thank you for your steady support. I gotta go."

"Football practice?"

"Yeah, but first I really gotta go."

I drink way too much water.

In the boys' room
(Only Boys Allowed In This Chapter)

Okay. I did my thing and I was washing my hands when I noticed Jack standing behind me, his head drenched. I looked to my left, and there was Mel—head drenched. I looked to my right, and there was Howie— same as Jack and Mel. Now if you were unfamiliar with Jon Scieszka Middle School, you might think that part of the daily tradition is sticking your entire head into a pail full of water. Not so, but close. As Jack, Howie, and Mel left the room, the horrific answer stood there smiling at me.

It was Todd Dornan, Scieszka's star quarterback, the most popular kid in school and my nemesis since kinder-garten. Next to him stood his goon and the team's mean-est lineman, the very large Milton Pierce. This was not good news.

"Hello, *Stacy*," said Todd.

"Todd. Milton. Well, as always, it's been an absolute pleasure. Gotta go."

As I attempted to leave, I ran right into Milton's extremely sizable chest.

"Stacy, Stacy, Stacy," said Todd. "You act as if you don't enjoy our company."

"Not enjoy your company? That is so laughable. Believe me, if it weren't for the fact that I am urgently needed at football practice, nothing would make me happier than to spend the rest of the day with you two."

Todd and Milton laughed so loud you would think that my being on the football team was a joke.

"You're the water boy," cackled Todd.

"Manager. I'm the team's manager."

Actually, while technically I was the manager, I was also the team's fifth-string defensive back. I had yet to actually get onto the field during a game, except when I brought out the water, but you never know. The fact that I was always in the wrong place at the wrong time and couldn't throw or catch very well seemed to negatively affect the coach's opinion of me. But just in case the first fourteen defensive backs on the team got hurt, I was always ready.

"Who is it that brings the water out to us players?" asked Milton.

"And you're saying that saving our team from becoming

dehydrated is unimportant? In fact, if I don't get over there right now, thirty-five players could end up passing out. Do you really want to be responsible for that?" I asked as I went for the door.

Still, Milton's chest wasn't budging.

"Stacy," Todd reminded me. "Are we forgetting about my test?"

How could I forget about something that happens every day?

"Good," said Todd, not waiting for my answer. "Here goes today's question. What is my favorite color?"

"I don't know. Fuschia?"

"That ain't no color," chimed in the ever-cerebral Milton.

"Oh. You were so close," said Todd. "The answer is white."

"But white isn't really one color," I said, trying to save myself. "It's actually the presence of all colors."

"You must think I'm an idiot," said Todd.

You have no idea how hard it was to hold my tongue.

"I guess we know the penalty for a wrong answer, don't we, Stacy?" said Todd as he smiled at Milton.

Unfortunately, I did.

EXITING the boys' room
(Girls Allowed Again)

As I exited the bathroom, head soaked, all I could think was:

At least they flushed first.

Still, I was yucky. In fact, I wouldn't read this too close if I were you. Why in the world ladies wear toilet water is beyond me.

10

tractor

"You stink, Little!" yelled out Coach Petercuskie.

"Coach, I'm trying as hard as I can."

"I'm not talking about your playing ability, though it is pretty bad. I'm talking about that smell. What did you do, take a bath in the toilet?"

Did I really have to answer?

"And you're late. These guys are thirsty."

"Coach, I am really sick of being your little slave. How about you telling these guys to get the stinkin' water themselves?"

At least, that's what I wanted to say. Instead, I went with the ever-popular:

"Sorry, sir. It won't happen again."

"After you bring out the water, I want you to get on

defense. We're a little short on players for Thinthith to run over."

Norman "Tractor" Thinthith was the biggest thirteen-year-old ever known to man. A seven-foot-tall, 375 pounds of hammering hurt. He might have been a bit smaller, but from ground level, he seemed pretty humongous. As good as he was, I don't remember if he was ever actually tackled. Oh, there were those people who tried to bring him down. Hospitals were full of them. As big as he was, Tractor was fast enough to run past any opposing player, but I think he had more fun going *through* them. I say "think" because it's not like he'd tell you. Tractor talked to no one, and the way he looked at you if you got near him, no one took a chance of talking to him.

Rumor was that every single kid who didn't go to Jon Scieszka Middle School didn't go there because he was dead. And they were *deaded* by Tractor. It's not like I knew for sure, but rumors don't lie.

"Hurry up, Little! Tractor needs some fresh meat!" yelled Coach Petercuskie.

I ran out onto the field. Not exactly ran. I was more dragged out there by three other players. They moved Tractor to defensive line—not part of the line—he was the entire line. I was placed in the offensive backfield where I would be most *offensive*.

The ball was snapped to Todd who, with a you're-dead

smile, handed it off to me. When Milton tried to block him, Tractor discarded Milton like a used tissue. There was nothing between Tractor and me but the ball.

With Godzilla ready to trample you like a small Japanese building, a lot of guys would run the opposite way. But I wanted to get into a real game in the worst way, and the only way I would ever get the chance was if I could show that I wasn't afraid. I mean, I was afraid, but I couldn't let Coach or Tractor know that. Hopefully neither of them noticed the fear written across my face. How Todd wrote it there without me noticing I'll never know.

I decided to run as hard as I could straight into Tractor's gut. If everything worked out the way I figured, Tractor would be so shocked that he would forget to tackle me and I would end up in the end zone.

That's the last thing I remember.

10 ¹/₂

knocked out

11

After the Smelling Salts

I limped home, knowing that my football strategy needed some rethinking. I also found out that I had yet to get rid of my rank toilet smell.

"Casey, do you have a fever?" said Mom. "You look flushed."

She didn't actually say that. I just couldn't resist. But with the toilet smell mixed with fresh football sweat, I did smell pretty bad. How bad? My mother made me eat dinner *in* the shower.

While there, I had an epiphany. I know what you're asking. What is an epiphany? Easy. An epiphany is a revelation. I'll save you asking the next question. A revelation is when you finally realize the answer to a question or a problem. Actually, I had two epiphanies. The first was that macaroni and cheese really loses its pizzazz when soaked in shower water. The second was the one that would change my life forever.

My epiphany: If I wanted to be on time, I needed something to remind me of what time it was.

My interruptive desire: Oh, if only something like that actually existed!

My epiphany resumes: There is something like that. It's called a watch.

My dad suggested that I go up to the attic, where we had a box of old watches that my grandfather used to tinker with. I might as well have not taken the shower. The dust was so thick up there, I needed a compass to find my nose.

I finally made my way to Grandpop Jesse's trunk, but I didn't have a key to open it. Luckily, it had no lid. After blowing off the dust and coughing up a tornado, I started going through a bunch of stuff, finally pulling out a picture of my grandfather standing next to some kind of weird clock contraption.

Written on the picture were these words:

Mike,
The doin' is in doin' for others or you ain't doin' nothin' at all.
Love, Dad

Mike is my dad.

Mixed in with a bunch of old parts, wires, and

miscellaneous junk were a whole lot of clocks and watches.

But what was really cool was an old notebook full of handwritten notes. The notebook made two things extremely clear. One, Grandpop had horrible handwriting. And two, he kept an old watch in a pocket inside the notebook. A watch! It was old, but it was, in fact, a watch. The answer to all my problems.

It was kind of weird looking, unlike any I had seen before. There was no stem to wind it (which you had to do with most old watches) but, surprisingly, it was ticking and telling time. I was finally going to get my life together. I would never be late again.

12

or maybe not

"You're late," said Dad.

I wasn't actually late, but Dad figured if he greeted me that way, he'd be right most of the time.

"Not anymore. Look at this," I said, showing off my new old watch.

"Nice, but if you're relying on that, I'd make sure I had a clock close by," said Dad. "It never worked right. Grandpop wore it everywhere but, then again, he never got anywhere on time."

I looked at the watch, and it was already running behind. I began to rethink my new positive attitude.

"Grandpop wasn't the best inventor," added Dad.

"What do you mean?"

"Ever hear of a Gas-a-nator?"

"A what?"

"A Gas-a-nator. The thing that changes water into gas."

"I didn't know you could do that."

"You can't. It's impossible. But 'impossible' wasn't in Grandpop's vocabulary. He built his Gas-a-nator."

"Didn't work?"

"It worked. Sort of. Made water flammable."

"That's pretty neat."

"Burned down his shop."

I figured I'd better get me another watch.

"Dad. What did Grandpop mean by 'The doin' is in doin' for others or you ain't doin' nothin' at all'?"

"Grandpop might have been a poor inventor, but he was one of the good guys."

"Like you," I added quickly and deftly.

(Note: Never miss an opportunity to score points with your parents. It distracts them from whatever they were mad at you for in the first place.)

"Thanks," said Dad. Then he hugged me.

Boy, I am good.

13

I slipped off my new, old, kind of broken watch, placed it on Grandpop's picture, and climbed into bed

I slipped off my new, old, kind of broken watch, placed it on Grandpop's picture, and climbed into bed.

Well, that was a waste of a perfectly good chapter.

14

A Chapter
Not to Be Wasted

"**C**asey Little! Wake up! You're going to be late for school!"

This time I had to agree. If only I had a watch that worked, instead of the one on . . . my wrist? Huh? How did it get on my wrist? I must have done one of those sleepwalking things where you get up during the night and do stuff you don't remember. I took it off, slid it back on Grandpop's picture, and got ready to go to school.

Mom, Dad, and my six-year-old sister, Kelly, were finishing breakfast as I got to the kitchen.

"So, you decided to wear the watch anyway," said Dad.

Huh? Holy moly. It was back on my wrist. Again.

"Um, yeah. You know. In honor of Grandpop."

I figured I had to lie. What was I going to say? "No, the

watch put itself on me"?

"Casey, I told you, that old watch will never get you anyplace on time," said Dad.

"Um. Listen, I'll be right back. I gotta check something."

"You're going to be late," said Mom.

"Thanks, Mom."

I ran back to the bedroom. No big deal really, except that maybe . . . Grandpop's old watch was **HAUNTED.**

the Go-back

Back in my room, I pulled out Grandpop's notebook and began flipping through the pages, looking to see how a watch was doing things that a watch shouldn't be allowed to do. I didn't know what was going on, but maybe Grandpop had an explanation.

And there it was. A drawing of the watch with Grandpop's scribbled notes right next to it.

The Go-back

No ordinary watch is this,
For it knows your will and more,
To take you back and fix the wrong,
Just fifteen minutes before.

WARNING!
You can go back in time, but not ahead.
DIRE WARNING!
The Go-back sometimes seems to have
a mind of its own.

"The Go-back," I said to no one in particular. "What a crock." That in itself was kind of weird, since I had no idea what a crock was.

16

Not such a crock

The weekend had finally come, the only thing I was never late for.

Dad and I sat in front of the television enjoying our Friday night ritual, watching *Quizzers*, our very favorite game show.

"When are you going to take off that broken old watch?" asked Dad.

"I've tried," I mumbled.

"What?"

"I, um, mean I *cried*—when I thought about taking it off. You know, it being Grandpop's and all."

I was just not a very good liar when put on the spot.

"The answer is: the first man to fly in a balloon," said Chet Balls, *Quizzers*'s well-groomed, ever-smiling host.

"Who is a very tiny person?" I answered.

"Who is Pierre LaPontz?" said the *Quizzers* contestant.

"Wrong," I said.

"That is correct," Balls corrected me.

"Of course," I said, slapping my head.

"Casey, you'd have to be a genius to get any of these right," said Dad, trying to reassure me that I wasn't a complete idiot.

"The answer is: an inflammation of the colon," offered Balls.

"What is . . . disgusting?" I said, cringing.

"What is diverticulitis?" answered the obviously incorrect contestant.

"Correct," said Balls.

I was pretty sure that diver-whatever was another word for "disgusting."

I glanced out the window and caught a glimpse of two of Jon Scieszka Middle School's most popular cheerleaders, Amy Anderson and Danielle Depardieu, strolling by the house. They think they're so hot. Of course, I'd have to agree with them. Not that I was interested in them. Not really. Well, hardly.

17

Really.
I Have No Interest
in Either of Them

I *nonchalantly* ran out of the house, attempting to look like I didn't even know that Amy and Danielle were there. Here's a tip: when you're trying to be nonchalant, don't run across a lawn that's been dug up for sewer repair.

Being extremely coordinated, I tripped over a large rock (that I'm sure jumped in front of me) and tumbled like a wayward football, landing at the feet of Danielle, the prettier one of the two girls I wasn't interested in. Now not only was I nervous, I was humiliated.

"Hi, Casey," said Danielle.

"Hi," I artfully countered.

"What are you doing?" asked Amy.

I kicked out my legs and sprang to my feet like a gymnast deserving a perfect ten. Well, at least a solid three.

"Training for the gymnastics team. I created that move myself. Looked like I fell down, didn't it? Pretty incredible, huh?"

"You have dog poop on your pants," pointed out the ever-observant Danielle.

"It's fake poop. I bought it for a magic trick I'm working on."

What a save.

"It smells like real dog poop." Amy scrunched her face to make that point perfectly clear.

"Um, that's because it's really good fake poop. It's very rare."

Change subject fast, Casey.

"I was thinking of maybe going to the Rebel Boys concert tonight."

"Oo-oo." Danielle cringed. "They're horrible."

"Yeah, that's why I decided to stay home," I quickly added. "Anyway, they've got that dopey band Vichyssoise opening up for them. Who can understand their stupid French, anyway?"

"I can." Danielle glared as if I had insulted her family or something. "My grandparents are from France."

And I didn't even have to lift my leg to put my foot in my mouth.

"Did I say 'French'? I meant 'stench.' Because their

stench is very bad . . . or good. Whatever makes me sound better."

"Huh?" said Danielle.

Hurry up. Someone pour water over me so I can melt away. (Hey, it worked in *The Wizard of Oz*.)

"Nice watch, Casey," said Amy without a hint of sincerity.

"I'm not wearing any . . ."

But I was wearing it . . . again.

"Oh, and it keeps such good time," Amy said, referring to the wrong time on the watch.

"Y'know, it's right at least twice a day."

I think the irony was lost on her.

"Casey! Come on in! You have to take a bath!"

Omigod. My mother had entered the why-don't-you-just-show-them-my-underwear zone.

"You better go in and let your mommy give you a bath," said Amy, smirking.

As they walked off giggling, I tried to save my honor.

"She wasn't talking to me," I called after them. "She was talking to my little brother . . . *Tracey*. My little *French* brother, Tracey. I don't take baths. In fact, I never wash myself at all."

Perhaps that didn't come out right. I'm pretty sure they began to giggle louder.

One last shot.

"I love French fries!"

Air ball.

As pitiful as pitiful could be, I headed for the house, making sure not to have eye contact with the newest member of my traitor list . . . Mom.

"Ugh, Casey," said Mom. "Did you soil something?"

"Just my reputation."

18

Yes, I Take Baths

You have no idea how the smell of dog poop on the outside of your pants can sink so deeply under your skin. But that wasn't the most startling discovery I made during my bath. The watch that I had again taken off and, in fact, locked in my drawer was once again on my wrist. And now a loud buzzing sound was coming from it.

"Casey," my mother yelled from downstairs, "are you using your dad's electric razor in the bathtub? You'll electrocute yourself."

"No, Mom, I'm just humming . . . *like* an electric razor."

I dipped my wrist under the water, hoping that I might be able to drown out the sound.

The water around my wrist began to swirl wildly. My

hand began to splash about uncontrollably as if I were a salmon just pulled from the water on its way upstream. I grabbed my arm with my other hand, trying to wrestle it to a stop, but my defiant appendage seemed to have a life of its own.

"Casey?"

My sister? In the bathroom? While I'm in the bath? Naked?

"Kelly! I'm taking a bath!"

I really have to remember to lock that door.

"You don't own the bathroom."

Six years old and she was already an expert in property law.

"Mom! Will you tell Kelly to get out of the bathroom!"

Just then my watch hand took a wild swing through the water, whipping a tidal wave onto my kid sister. Cool.

"Mom! Casey's trying to drown me!"

"What is going on in here?"

Great. Now two females staring at my nakedness.

"Mom. Please. How about some privacy?" I pleaded. "I'm trying to take a bath, and the water's getting cold."

"It looks more like you're trying to drown your sister."

And before I could defend myself, my watch hand snapped back. Though I tried mightily to hold it still, it gathered another large scoop of water and swept a deluge, drenching my mom. To say that she was absolutely shocked by what I did is, well, to say the absolute truth. I awaited the eruption. It's pretty amazing that though she had just been dowsed with cold water, I could see volcanic heat building up behind a brilliant red glow on her face.

"Well, you, mister, have just lost Nintendo privileges for the year."

Okay. Maybe it's not as bad as it sounds. I mean, did she mean for the rest of *this* year, which only had a couple of months left, or did it mean a full year starting from now?

"And that means a full year, young man."

A life sentence—

"And I'm sending your father up."

—jacked up to death.

19

What's the BUZZ?

Mom and Kelly left the bathroom and I got out of the water, or what was left of the water. As strange as things had been up to now, they were about to get even stranger. As I was drying off . . .

B-U-U-Z-Z-Z-Z.

Huh?

Suddenly the watch face flipped open, revealing another kind of neat, digital watch underneath.

Cool!

The number 10 blinked, then 9, then 8, and then—

In my head flashed Grandpop's note:

> No ordinary watch is this,
> For it knows your will and more,

To take you back and fix the wrong,
Just fifteen minutes before.

"Holy—"

SWOOSH!

WOW!

*S*WOOSH!
 Okay. Now this is going to be hard to believe. I mean, why would you believe it? I don't know if I believe it . . . even now.

I was no longer in the bath. I wasn't even in the bathroom! And, thankfully, I wasn't naked. I was sitting in the living room watching *Quizzers* with Dad. Had I dreamed about the whole bathroom thing? Was talking to Amy and Danielle just a dream? What about losing Nintendo? Or was I dreaming now? Not that a dream about watching *Quizzers* is such a special dream.

What the heck was happening? I was starting to get dizzy. Not the good kind, like from a roller coaster, but dizzy like from trying to learn algebra.

"You okay, boy?" asked Dad.

"Uh, yeah. What day is it?"

"It's Friday, son. Why?"

"Just wanted to make sure you knew."

And what I heard on the TV confirmed that I must be going nuts.

"The answer is: the first man to fly in a balloon," said Chet Balls, *Quizzers*'s well-groomed, ever-smiling host.

"Uh, who is Pierre LaPontz?" I muttered automatically. Dad smirked.

"Who is Pierre LaPontz?" said the *Quizzers* contestant. Dad raised a brow.

I was, I must say, intrigued.

"Good guess, Case."

"Uh, yeah. Guess." Then, to myself, "Oh, man. Oh, man. Oh, man."

"Calm down, son. You only got one right."

My excitement was louder than I thought.

"Yeah. Dad, be totally honest with me. Are you in my dream?"

"What?"

"The answer is: an inflammation of the colon," offered Balls.

Well, here goes.

"What is diverticulitis?"

"What is diverticulitis?" answered the contestant.

"Correct," said Balls.

"Yes!" I cheered myself.

"How did you . . . ?" asked Dad.

"Dad, some things are better left unanswered."

Mostly because I had no idea how to answer the question myself. But to myself I was saying, "How cool is this!"

Out the window, Danielle and Amy were just approaching . . . again. Right on time.

"Excuse me for a second, Dad."

I ran outside and left Dad to question life and my new part in it.

21

Parlez-Vous Français?

I hurried out of the house and quickly put on the brakes. As you already know, the lawn was in the midst of being dug up. And now, with just a little skip to the right, I missed the large rock and *le poop* entirely. I stationed myself strategically as the girls approached.

"Hi, Casey," said Danielle.

"Hey, Casey," said Amy.

I took a deep breath. If I was wrong, I would be even more of a jerk than I was before, if there was a *before*. If I was right—well, if I was right, I was just about to find out.

"*Bonsoir*, ladies."

"You speak French?" asked Danielle.

"Yes, *bonsoir*. I speak a little. In fact, I love everything French. Including anyone who might be related to anyone

French. You see, my ancestors came over from France."

"Omigod. So did mine! Wow. This is so neat. I didn't know 'Casey' was a French name."

"Oh yeah. The proper pronunciation is (French accent) 'Ca-*say*.' I only pronounce it 'Casey' to fit in. You know. To make those who aren't *bi-literal* feel comfort-able."

"What part of France did your people come from?"

"Um . . . the suburbs."

"Oh."

"Yep. I was even thinking of going to the Vichyssoise concert tonight. Unfortunately, those disgusting Rebel Boys are on the same bill. I can't stand them."

"Me neither," agreed Danielle.

Man. This is so-o-o great.

"Casey!" my mother yelled. "Come on in! You have to take—"

"No need to yell, Madame," I interrupted cooly. "I'll be there in a second."

And then to the girls, "My mom needs help with her . . . escargot."

I figured I'd go all the way.

"It's my recipe."

"You make escargot, too?" swooned Danielle.

"*Bonsoir*," I confirmed, hoping that escargot was actu-ally some kind of food.

"I just love snails with garlic," said Danielle.

"Me too," I said, nearly choking. "But not nearly as much as escargot."

Danielle looked at me kind of oddly.

"Listen, we gotta go," said Amy.

"See you at school on Monday?" asked Danielle.

With my best French accent: "But of course."

As the girls walked out of sight, I smiled toward the heavens.

"Thanks, Grandpop."

And from that point on, my life as I had known it would be completely different. Everything, I thought, would be as wonderful as wonderful could be. Unfortunately, however, the Go-back had other plans.

on time . . . or Not

That Monday morning, with the Go-back clasped to my wrist, I raced to school. I had yet to figure out how to get it to work or know when it would work on its own. Worse, it didn't exactly keep great time. Why would I expect a time machine that didn't seem to work all that well to keep the right time?

I screeched to a stop as Nina was about to walk into school.

"Hel-loooo, Nina."

"You've got to be kidding. Do you know what time it is?" she said as she walked in.

"Yeah. Not late."

RI-I-ING!

Drat.

As I finished locking my bike, I knew for sure that I would finally be on—

"Hello, Stacy."

Then again.

"Test time," reminded a diabolically smiling Todd.

"Isn't it a little early for this?"

"I'm overbooked today," said the exceptionally busy bully. "I wanted to get this out of the way as soon as I could."

"Come on, guys. If I'm not on time, I'm going to be in a lot of trouble."

"Oh my. I didn't realize that. Can you ever forgive me?"

"Of course I can forgive you. See ya."

I got a good two feet away before Milton's massive arm latched on to my shoulder.

"The test," said Milton.

"Oh, right. Forgot."

"Let me see. I'll make it an easy one. Who is my favorite singing group?" Todd asked.

"Oh, I don't know. Your stinkin' ugly face?"

"What?" asked the surprised bully.

"Come on, Todd. Your Stinkin' Ugly Face is the hottest new rap group in the country."

Didn't know if he was stupid enough to believe that but . . .

"Oh yeah, right," Todd nodded. "I knew that."

"Yeah, they're pretty good," added Milton Einstein.

"But still wrong," said Todd. "My favorite group is the Philadelphia Phillies."

"That's a baseball team."

"Yeah, so?"

"But you said . . ."

"Yeah . . . ?"

"Never mind."

23

FlUShed Again

After our quick Stop & Dunk in the boys' room, I headed to homeroom, drenched and late. One thing kept running through my mind: I really have to start studying for Todd's tests. "Good afternoon, Mr. Little," said Ms. Loozer.

Afternoon? Man, I was really late. Then again, I think she was making a point.

Nina just shook her head.

"I think Principal Gordon would like to see you," said Ms. Loozer.

As many times as I've been sent to Gordon's office, you would think he would be tired of seeing me already. As I made an about-face to leave, I looked at the Go-back and knew that Dad was right. I couldn't rely on it . . . especially now, when I really could use it.

I left for Principal Gordon's office and immediately realized that I wouldn't have to go all the way down there.

"What are you doing in the hallway during class, Mr. Little?"

How nice it was that Gordon thought enough to come and meet me.

"I'm waiting."

Before I could answer, Mr. Gordon, who seemed to be great at reading minds, read mine.

"Let me guess. You're in the hallway because you were late again and you were on your way to see me."

"Kind of," I said, hoping he would say it was unnecessary to go all the way down to his office because he was going to give me one more chance.

"Do you know how to spell 'suspension,' Mr. Little?"

"S-u-s-p-e—"

"I know how to spell it, Mr. Little, but you, my late friend, are going to live it."

And before I could say another smart-alecky thing that would get me in even more trouble . . .

BU-UZ-Z-Z-Z!

"What is that?" asked Principal Gordon.

"Um, nothing," I said as I unsuccessfully attempted to hold my arm down. My arm decided it wanted to do a windmill impression. The Go-back was doing its thing.

"Is that supposed to be funny, Mr. Little?" said Principal Gordon.

Wait a minute, I thought. If this meant I was going back in time again, then what was happening at that point would have never happened.

"I'm waiting for an explanation," demanded Gordon. "That is, unless you'd like to be suspended for the rest of the year."

"I sure hope this is working," I said quietly.

"What was that?"

Obviously I didn't say it quietly enough. But as I watched the Go-back counting down, I thought, Here goes nothing.

"I said, 'You, Principal Gordon, have the worst breath in the history of the world.'"

He looked at me as if I had just blown my nose on his tie. I thought about it, but held back on that one.

Instead I went with something I'd wanted to say for a long time.

"If the army had your breath, we'd never need bombs."

"What makes you think you can get away with this disrespect?" asked the enraged Gordon.

"I'm thinking luck. And a whole bunch of stupidity."

SWOOSH!

FIFTEEN MINUTES EARLIER

*I-I-ING!*
Drat.

But wait. *It worked!* It was fifteen minutes before. I mean it was now, but a now that was fifteen minutes earlier than the old now. The old now that never existed.

"Hello, Stacy."

Never have I been so glad to hear Todd's voice.

"Test time," reminded the diabolically smiling Todd . . . again, sort of.

"Boy, am I glad you showed up early," I said, hardly able to restrain my joy. "I figured you might be really busy today, so I wanted to help you get this out of the way as soon as I could."

The look on Todd's face was priceless. Well, not really.

You probably could get it for under a dollar fifty on eBay.

Milton's massive arm latched on to my shoulder.

"You trying to be a wise guy?" asked Milton.

"I don't really have to try. I'm already pretty good at it."

"I'm in a hurry," said Todd. "Let's do this."

"Can't wait."

"All right. Let me see. I'll make it an easy one. Who is my favorite singing group?"

"Um. Before I guess, could you do me a small favor?"

"Like what?"

"How about writing the answer down? You know, not that you would do it. But, you know, some guys might tell me I'm wrong even if I get it right."

"You callin' me a liar?"

"Look. I'm a jerky little creep. Just humor me."

So Todd wrote it down. Thank you, God.

"Could you hurry up," I urged. "I need that head flush bad."

Todd handed the paper to Milton.

"Okay, note boy," he said as he winked at Milton. "Who's my favorite group?"

"You know, there's a lot of great groups," I said. "There were the Beatles. There were the Cockroaches. And will we ever forget You Two Gotta Be the Ugliest Boneheads in the World?"

"What?"

"You Two Gotta Be the Ugliest Boneheads in the World," I repeated with the utmost delight. "You know, that great new rap group?"

"Oh yeah. Sure. They're pretty good," agreed Todd Bonehead. "Now cut the stalling, jerk boy. Who's my favorite group?"

"Hmm. I'll go with a long shot. The Philadelphia Phillies."

"Hah, You guessed wro . . . Hey."

I grabbed the paper from the stunned Milton's hands and opened it.

"Well, what do you know? I was right. What a lucky guess. Guess I'll have to miss the flush. See ya later."

"I don't know how you did whatever it is that you did," blared a raging Todd, "but I swear, I won't forget it."

As I strutted into the school, leaving those clods standing there, mouths hanging open, looking even dumber than before, I knew the Go-back and I were going to be great pals.

25

I've Got to Tell Someone

I kind of felt like I was Clark Kent and I couldn't tell anyone that I was really Superman. Or was it that I felt like Superman, but I couldn't tell anyone I was Clark Kent? It was starting to get confusing.

"Hey, Case. You gonna eat your French fries?"

Nina is such a mooch.

"Why don't you buy your own fries?"

"Why should I if you're not eating yours?"

"When don't I eat them?"

"I just thought that you were thinking that I was such a good friend that you wanted to show me just how much by giving me your fries."

"You're not that good a friend."

Then Nina made this face where she sticks out her

bottom lip about a mile and makes it quiver. I know she's not really sad, but you have to see this face. She thinks she can get me to do anything. It's pathetic.

"Okay, you can have half," I said grudgingly.

"Yes!"

She is such a mooch.

"How'd you ever manage to get to school on time today? Your mother use a crane to lift you out of bed?"

"Well, it's kind of a secret."

There was the pathetic face again.

"Come on, Nina. I really can't tell."

Even more face.

"I tell you all my secrets," said Nina.

"You're a girl. You tell everyone your secrets."

"Okay, I'll tell you. But you have to promise not to tell anyone else."

"I promise," she said, crossing her heart.

"No. Not just a cross-your-heart promise. It's got to be one of those If I tell anyone I'll run naked all through school yelling, 'Look at me, I'm a duck.'"

"Casey."

I looked around the McDonald's, checking out the noise level, making sure it was loud enough so no one else could hear.

"Here's how I did it."

I held up my wrist.

"You came to school on time because you have a wrist?"

Duh. I held up the wrong hand.

"No, this," I said, holding up the Go-back wrist.

"That's it? You got to school on time because of an old watch?"

She looked closer.

"It doesn't even have the right time."

I looked around once more, then leaned in closer to Nina.

"It's a time machine."

"What do you mean, 'time machine'?"

"Time machine. Like in the movies. You know. The kind of thing that takes you back in time."

"Come on."

"I'm serious. This is a time machine."

"Yeah. Okay, Case. If it's a time machine, prove it. Let's go back and find out if Ben Franklin really flew a kite to discover electricity."

"Um. It's not really one of those good ones that can go back to Ben Franklin or dinosaurs or really far back times like that."

"Okay, then. How about if we go back to when man first walked on the moon? That'd be cool."

"Too far."

"How about yesterday?"

"Mmm. Nope."

"Exactly how far back can your so-called time machine go?"

"Um. Fifteen minutes."

"Wow, that is so neat. You mean we can actually go back to see what it was like when we first ordered lunch? Absolutely amazing."

So skeptical.

"Is it limited to fifteen minutes into the future?"

"Um. No."

"Well, at least we can find out what the world will be like in—"

"It doesn't go into the future at all."

"Let me get this straight. This thing on your wrist is a time machine, but it can only go back in time fifteen minutes and it doesn't go into the future at all?"

"That's about it."

"What idiot invented that?"

"My grandfather."

At least that shut her up . . . for a second.

"I'm sorry. I didn't mean—"

"Nina. He invented a thing that goes back in time. So what if it's only fifteen minutes? Inventing anything that goes back any amount of time . . . that's pretty cool."

"Yuh. If it really does that."

"It does. I swear."

"Then do it. Let's go back fifteen minutes."

"Uh. I can't make it work. It only goes back when it wants to."

"I see. So it also has a brain."

"Kind of."

"So, what do we do, just wait until its brain thinks it's time to go back?"

"That's about it."

"Okay. Where's the camera? We're on the *Make an Idiot out of Your Friend* show, aren't we?"

I felt like the idiot. How could I prove to her that the Go-back really works if . . .

Bu-uzz.

And the lid popped open.

"What was that? What's happening to your watch?" asked Nina.

All right! The Go-back was doing its thing.

"See. I told you I was telling you the truth."

7-6-5-4 . . .

"Casey, that is so cool. Does it mean that it's going to go back now?"

3-2-1

"Just watch."

SW . . .

Finally, I Have Proof

... *OOSH!*

"Order already, Case," said Nina.

Wow. Back at the McDonald's counter.

"Didja see, Nina? It works."

"What works?

"The Go-back."

"What's a Go-back?"

"It's the time mach—"

That's when it hit me. It worked, but only on me. Since I was the only one touching the Go-back, I was the only one who was aware that the entire world had just gone back in time.

"Well, if you're not going to order, nuthead, I will. I'll have a chicken sandwich and a medium cola."

"You want French fries with that?" asked the well-trained counter person.

"Nah. I'm not that hungry."

It was going to be a long lunch.

27

Big News About Something Really Small

I sat in my room reading Grandpop's notes over and over. No matter how many times I read them, it was very clear that the Go-back had a mind of its own. The Go-back alone would decide if and when it would go back.

That's when I noticed that there was another page stuck behind the one I was reading. I separated the two and that's when I saw . . . **THE BLOOD!**

Wow. Freaky. I'm looking at Grandpop's blood from who knows how many years ago. I wondered what horribleness must have taken place way back then. Amazing. Even while he was injured, it didn't stop Grandpop from crawling to his notepad to write down information that was important to him. What courage. What focus. What a guy.

That's when I smelled something familiar. A smell that reminded me of jelly. Strawberry jelly. It wasn't blood at all. It was old strawberry jelly that had made his notes stick together. Grandpop must have been eating jelly while he was working on the Go-back. Still, he had to be pretty focused to be able to eat and work at the same time.

I continued to read the jelly-stained notes.

The Other Side of the Go-back

If you turn it over to the other side,
A way for you will be shown,
To take a turnabout time-travel ride,
And Go-back fifteen minutes
when you choose.

As I sat there polishing the Go-back, all I kept thinking was, Grandpop was an even lousier poet than he was an inventor. And he didn't keep his stuff very neat. There was more dirt and grime stuck to the back of this thing than . . .

Holy moly. Underneath all the muck there was something. Something engraved.

Push this to go back in time. 👉 ⚪

And the finger pointed to a tiny little button right next to it.

Come on. That couldn't be what I thought it was . . . could it?

Well, there was only one way to find out.

28

And Find Out I Did

I met Nina at our town's famous man-made Le Natural Faux Lake Park.

"Do you know how crazy you've been acting lately?" Nina asked.

Unfortunately, I did, but I certainly wasn't going to let her know.

"Do you believe in time travel?" I asked, hoping she wouldn't think that I was a total jerk.

"For real?"

"No, for fake. Of course for real."

"I can picture time travel. I mean, I know that time flies." That's when she burst out laughing. That girl really breaks herself up.

"Very funny. What would you say if I could prove that time travel was possible?" I asked.

"I'd say, put up or shut up."

"Don't rush me. I'll show you, but you have to do exactly what I say."

"There're no wedgies involved here, right?"

"No wedgies."

We had just made a deal that could not be broken by man or dog.

"This is going to take about eighteen minutes."

"All right," she said, rolling her eyes.

"First, you have to write down three things that I couldn't possibly know."

"Is this a trick to find out stuff about me that you're going to end up blackmailing me with later?"

"Just write down things that you wouldn't mind me knowing."

She smirked, then wrote them down.

"Okay. Don't tell me what you wrote."

"How does this prove you can travel in time?"

"Now tell me what you wrote."

"You're nuts."

"Just tell me what you wrote."

"Okay. My first dog's name was Pizza."

"That's one."

"When I was three years old, I swallowed a nickel."

"Everything come out okay?"

I couldn't resist.

"Ow!"

And Nina couldn't resist punching me in the arm harder than a girl should be allowed to punch.

"Sorry. Okay. Last one?"

Time was running short.

"I think you have great hair."

A little bit embarrassing, but my hair did look pretty good that day.

"Now what?"

"Now we wait."

I checked the time on the Go-back. "Fourteen minutes."

"I don't get—"

"Just do what I say. You promised."

We stared at each other for fourteen minutes, then . . .

29

FOUrteen Minutes IS a REally LONG Time When YOU'VE GOt NOthing to DO but Wait

The fourteen minutes were up.

"Now watch this."

I hoped my math was right. I turned the Go-back over and pushed the little button, where it said—

Push this to go back in time.

10-9-8-7-6-5-4-3-

And still Nina smirked.

"Cute. But that doesn't mean—"

SWOOSH!

There we were. Fifteen minutes earlier.

"There're no wedgies involved here, right?"

"No wedgies."

"All right," she said, rolling her eyes.

"First, you have to write down three things that I couldn't possibly know."

"Is this a trick to find out stuff about me that you're going to end up blackmailing me with later?"

"Just write down things that you wouldn't mind me knowing."

She smirked, then wrote them down.

"Okay. Don't tell me what you wrote."

"How does this prove you can travel in time?"

"Because I'm going to tell you what those three things are."

"You're nuts. Go ahead. Tell me."

"Okay. Your first dog's name was Pizza."

She was stunned.

"You talked to my mother, right?"

"Even if I did, how would I know that would be the first thing you wrote?"

"Yeah, well . . ."

She held the paper tightly to her chest.

"What's the second one?"

"When you were three years old, you swallowed a nickel."

Nina's *stunned* turned to *flabbergasted*.

"This is some kind of trick, right?"

"Yeah, it's a trick. Just like you thinking that I have great hair is a trick."

Nina dropped the paper to the ground. A second later Nina dropped to the ground.

"How did you do that?"

"Just like I said. Fifteen minutes ago you told me those three things. Then I waited fifteen minutes and used the Go-back. It's hard to explain, but it doesn't matter how you explain it, it's just good old-fashioned time travel."

"That doesn't prove you can go back in time. Maybe you just read my mind. Or you could see through my hands to the paper."

"Yeah, right. You believe that I could read your mind or that I have X-ray vision, but time travel you can't believe."

I think that got her. She just sat there shaking her head.

Then, after about a minute, she looked up at me and smiled broadly.

"Cool. How about letting me try it?"

"I don't know. It seems like that would be kind of weird."

"Weird? You've got a time machine, Case. It doesn't get much weirder than that."

"I'm just not sure yet whether I'm allowed to let anyone else use it."

"Are you saying the time machine tells you what to do?"

"Kind of."

"I'm sorry. What planet did you say you were from?"

"Look. My mom and dad will be out tonight. Come on over, and I'll think about letting you try it."

"I'm there," she said, beaming.

"Remember, I only said I'd think about it."

And already I was thinking I might be making a big mistake.

30

Nervous Doesn't Mean Scared, Okay?

I kind of had an ulterior motive for asking Nina to come over. It seems like Mom and Dad's anniversary happens pretty much every year. And as always, they were going out to celebrate. I'm not sure exactly how they celebrate because they always leave Kelly and me at home . . . with a babysitter. But this anniversary Mom and Dad decided that, at almost thirteen, I was old enough to stay home and watch Kelly.

Of course, I could have started staying home alone without a babysitter years ago. I mean, it's not like I'm one of those scaredy-cat guys. But if I had stayed alone all those years, do you know how many babysitters would have gone broke? I just didn't want to be responsible for that.

And to prove that I had no problem staying alone, I

would have Nina there to watch how fearless I was. You know. Just in case someone needed verification of my lack of fear, it always helps to have a witness.

Geez, it was quiet. Too quiet, if you ask me.

Outside it was dark. Too dark, if you ask me.

Inside there was furniture. Too much furniture, whether you ask me or not.

Maybe I was thinking a little too much, but it didn't mean I was afraid. It only meant I was, um, thoughtful. Thoughtful enough to think about waking Kelly to sit with me just in case she was a little frightened sleeping in the house without Mom, Dad, or a babysitter.

What was taking Nina so long? A person can get pretty darn nervous waiting for someone to come over to verify just how *not nervous* he is.

"Hey! How about opening the door!" Nina yelled from outside.

I had been so busy talking to myself, I didn't even hear her knock.

"Hey, Nin."

"Took you long enough. Do you know how dark it is out there?"

"Didn't even notice. Come on in."

Even before she came into the living room, she got right down to business.

"So, let's get to it," she said.

"Get to what?" I said, figuring that my clever questioning would throw her off from trying the Go-back.

"Don't play stupid. Your time-machine thingy."

"Y'know, Nin, I don't know if it's such a good idea for you to try it. What if the Go-back doesn't want to . . . ?"

And that's when the Go-back showed it definitely had a mind of its own.

"Um, ignore what I just said, Nin."

"What do you mean?"

"Look at your wrist."

The Go-back was now on Nina's wrist.

"Wow. How did that get there?" asked Nina.

"I have no idea, but I'm thinking it means it'd be okay for you to try it."

"You mean it likes me?"

"Something like that . . . I guess."

"What do I have to do?"

"Let's try this. I'll tell you something that you wouldn't know about me. Like, say, last night I dreamed that a grilled cheese sandwich ate me for dinner."

"You must be very tasty."

"I've always thought of myself as refreshingly minty. Now let's wait about fourteen minutes and then you push the Go-back. That way, when you come back and tell me about the grilled cheese, I'll know that you actually went back."

"Gotcha."

We sat on the couch for what I have to say was a pretty boring fourteen minutes, then . . .

"Okay," I said. "Press it!"

And she did.

SWOOSH!

Nina Joins the Club

"Let's try this. I'll tell you something that you wouldn't know about me. Like, say, last night I dreamed that a—"

"Grilled cheese sandwich ate you for dinner," interrupted Nina.

"Huh? How did you know?"

"Because you told me fifteen minutes ago."

"Huh?"

"You told me that so that when I went back fifteen minutes, you would know that I went back."

"Holy moly," I said. "Then you . . ."

Nina winked.

"Cool," I said, surprised and a little relieved that I wasn't alone anymore.

"Way cool!" said Nina. "I want to do it again."

"Whoa. Let's not go crazy. I don't know how much *going back* is in there. We don't want to waste any of it."

"You worry too much."

"It's what I'm best at," I admitted.

"Do you realize what we can accomplish with this?"

"You mean besides knowing what food tends to devour me in my dreams?"

Still, I knew whatever I did, I should make sure I didn't do it selfishly.

Then again . . .

I'm Gonna Be Rich!

*L*ike you wouldn't do the same thing.

For example, with the Go-back I could make a killing in the stock market. That is, if I knew how the stock market worked.

Or I could see which horse wins a race then go back and bet on it. But I'm not allowed to gamble.

I could go back and buy a company pretty cheap that I knew was going to become real successful. But I could only go back fifteen minutes, not fifteen years.

This might not be as easy as I thought.

Tell me, if *you* had the Go-back, what would *you* do with it?

33

Your Ideas Here

This is your chapter. Get a separate piece of paper and write down as many things as you can about what you would do if you had a Go-back. I'll wait.

Casey

34

those were pretty Good ideas, but what about the Greater Good?

So, you would use it to win stuff, huh? Wouldn't that be cheating? I don't know if I'd go there. When I woke up the next morning, I was determined to right all the wrongs done . . . to me. And if I happened to pick up some fringe benefits along the way, so be it.

Mom made my favorite breakfast . . . banana, peanut butter, and chocolate-chip pancakes. I ate 'em until I couldn't fit another one in. Then, thanks to the Go-back, I ate them again . . . and again, so many times that I lost count. Funny, though, after a while, even though I love banana, peanut butter, and chocolate-chip pancakes, they started to taste kind of boring.

After breakfast I decided to really see what the Go-back could do.

As usual I was late for school, but after going back a few dozen times, I straightened that out.

I ran into some girls and was able to wow them with my ability to say just the right thing. 'Course, the whole redoing fifteen minutes just to get the last few seconds anywhere close to what I wanted was getting a little, um, repetitious.

Me: Hey, you lucky girls. I'm here.

The Lucky Girls: And we are out of here.

Me: Um . . . see ya.

SWOOSH!

Me: Lookin' good, ladies.

Ladies: Who do you think you are?

Me: I'm, uh . . .

SWOOSH!

Me: Hi.

Them: Hi.

It's gonna take a while to get this down.

But I was able to get Todd and Milton severely confused and awesomely upset because they were unable to give me the old toilet dip. Man, I was on top of the world.

And then it was time to really get to work.

"It is so nice to see you've made it on time, Mr. Little," said Ms. Loozer.

"Why, thank you, Ms. Loozer. I plan to make it a habit."

"That would be wonderful," said Ms. Loozer.

"Hopefully, you can also make a habit of getting better grades, starting with today's test."

"Test?"

"You forgot about the test?" she asked.

"Noo-oo. I'd never forget about the test. Um, remind me again. What is the test on?"

"History," she said, shaking her head.

"Yes. That's right. History. Um, history of what?"

"Does it really matter?"

No. It didn't matter, I didn't remember, and I didn't study.

"Okay," said Ms. Loozer, "despite Mr. Little's comedy routine, we will be getting started with the test."

She handed out the toughest twenty-question U.S. history test ever given to man or boy, or girl, for that matter. There were questions about presidents I never heard of. I mean, come on, a president named Chester Arthur? Then there were dates on which we supposedly had wars I never heard of; inventions that had no use; and famous slogans that were so famous I don't think anyone ever actually used them. No one would be able to pass this test, except maybe Nervous Pervis, who got an A on every test. If it weren't for the fact that it was multiple choice, I wouldn't have been able to fake an answer. Thankfully, it was over fast. How fast? No more than—you guessed it—around fifteen minutes.

"Okay. Pencils down. Hand your papers forward."

I thought about that a good half a second.

As Ms. Loozer was collecting the papers, I jumped up and grabbed Nervous Pervis's test off her desk.

"Hey!" screamed Pervis.

"Don't worry, Perv," I assured her. "You'll get it right the next time you take it."

"Next time?" she said. "What are you talking about?"

I studied the answer list, concentrating as hard as I could. I tried to make the multiple choice letters into a word: ABACCEDACEDABEDACEDE. That was much too long to memorize.

"Mr. Little! What do you think you're doing?" scolded Ms. Loozer.

It is especially hard trying to memorize while your teacher is chasing you around the room.

"Casey! Give me that paper right this minute!"

Maybe if I could break it into two words, it would be easier: ABACCEDACE and DABEDACEDE.

"I'm warning you, Mr. Little. If you don't hand me that paper right now—"

Maybe four words would work.

ABACC EDACE DABED ACEDE. ABACC EDACE DABED ACEDE. ABACC EDACE DABED ACEDE.

I got it. And not a second too soon, because not only was Ms. Loozer bearing down on me, so was fifteen minutes.

Ms. Loozer grabbed me, and the paper, just as I pressed
the . . .

SWOOSH!

Almost on cue, Ms. Loozer handed out the same tough
U.S. history test ever given to man. I wrote down all twenty
answers before she finished passing out the test.

ABACC EDACE DABED ACEDE. Did four ridicu-
lous words ever sound better? I pretended I was still writing them down as Ms. Loozer gave the test. Didn't want to
be too obvious.

"Okay. Pencils down. Hand your papers forward."

And I did.

"Mr. Little. You seem very proud of yourself," said Ms.
Loozer. "Was there an answer you actually knew?"

"Not one," I said, not letting a hint of irony shine
through.

She took a look at my paper.

"Well, I see you literally answered all the questions."

"I tried my best," I said. "I can't do any more than that."

"Why do you have to be such a wise guy?" whispered
Nina.

"Because I am one?"

"It might be okay for you to act like that if you were
actually passing, Case, but your grades are about ready to
fall off the ends of the earth."

"Nin, didn't you have enough time to study? The earth
isn't flat. My grades can't fall off. They might go rolling

round and round the earth's circumference, but 'fall off the earth'? You make me laugh."

As Ms. Loozer looked at my paper, an expression crossed her face that I had never seen before . . . at least when a teacher graded my tests. Bewilderment. As if in a daze, she wandered to her desk, took out a scoring sheet and, as she checked my answers, her expression changed from bewilderment to . . . even more bewildered (I have to get myself a thesaurus).

"Mr. Little. I see that you finally found the time to prepare for a test."

"Twice the normal time."

"Class. It is my privilege to say something I never thought I would ever say in this class. Casey Little scored one hundred percent."

The entire class erupted into applause, except for Nina, who squinted skeptically.

"And my guess," added Ms. Loozer, "is that I'll never be saying that again."

Wanna bet?

SWOOSH!

And about fourteen minutes later . . .

"Class. It is my privilege to say something I never thought I would ever say in this class. Casey Little scored one hundred percent."

Is this fun or what?

35

I Think I May Actually Be Getting Better Looking

"**Y**ou used the Go-back, didn't you?" grilled Nina the nonbeliever between bites of her lunch burrito.

"Are you saying that you don't think I could ace a test without cheating?"

"Exactly."

"You are so—right!"

"Do you think that's the way your grandfather would have wanted you to use the Go-back?"

"My grandpop would have wanted me to be happy, and this makes me happy."

Jack, Howie, and Mel, all with soaked heads, sat down.

"Flunk Dornan's test again?"

"How come you're getting away without Todd and Milton dunking you?" asked Howie.

"Timing," I said. "You either got it or you don't."

"I'd call it baloney," chimed in Nina.

"Stop making me hungry." I was just so darn funny.

"*Bonjour*, Casey."

It was Danielle Depardieu.

"*Bon*-yourself, Danielle," I responded ever so cleverly.

"When did you learn to start speaking French so badly?" asked Nina.

"Part of my timing."

"What are you doing hanging around the losers, Danielle?" interrupted Todd, who unfortunately showed up right behind Danielle.

"Lay off him, Todd," insisted Danielle. "He's French."

"He's not French. He's Caucasian," said Todd the bona-fide idiot.

"Yeah. I'm pretty sure both his parents are from Caucasia," said Milton the way-more-than-bona-fide idiot.

All of a sudden the lunchroom went pitch black—like a total eclipse of the sun. Except there was no sun. It was a total eclipse of Tractor Thinthith. The room was silent as the largest hunk of boy at Scieszka stood at the entrance to the lunchroom, filling the doorway from side to side and top to bottom, blocking any light from the hall.

He walked over to the only empty table. *Tractor's table.* No one else dared sit there. He sat down, opened his half-gallon carton of milk, and guzzled it in one swallow. Everyone in the room let out a collective sigh, as if the fact that he didn't break anyone's neck on the way to his table was a victory. As everyone in the cafeteria began to talk again, I thought I detected a smidgen of a smile on Tractor's face. I had never seen him smile before, so I couldn't be sure. It was as if he got a kick out of the effect he had on everyone. Even though no one had actually ever witnessed any of the terror he had supposedly unleashed, no one was willing to take the chance of testing him.

"Man, that guy may be the best football player in the world, but he is one strange dude," said Todd.

"Why don't you tell him that?" asked Amy.

"'Cause he wants to see tomorrow," said Nina.

"Anyone know why he's always alone?" I asked.

"He lives with his grandmother," said Howie.

"I heard that he killed his parents," whispered Milton.

"Then why isn't he in jail?" I asked.

"They say he murdered the cops who tried to arrest him," said Danielle.

Just then Tractor got up and came toward our table. As he was about to pass by, he turned right into Milton's face.

"Boo!" whispered Tractor.

Milton fell backward, rolling up into a ball under the table, trembling like a leaf in a windstorm. Tractor strolled away. This time I was sure he was smiling.

Fifteen Minutes-
of practice

"Since when do you wear a watch to practice?" asked Coach Petercuskie.

"I'm trying to get my timing down."

Of course he had no idea what I was talking about, but I figured if the opportunity arose, maybe I'd give a shot at seeing how the Go-back might make me a better player. Of course, it's all about raw talent, but it doesn't hurt to back that up with, um, good timing.

"Okay, Little. Go in for Brosnan. No use hurting the regulars right before the big play-off game."

I ran in, not really sure how I would be able to use the Go-back to my advantage.

"Hey, Stacy," said the oh-so-hysterical Todd. "Ready to get pummeled?"

I lined up on defense, guarding Broderick "Broad"

Miller, one of our fastest receivers. There was no way I could normally cover him . . . at least the *first time*.

The ball was centered, and Miller zigged and zagged as he ran to his predetermined spot fifteen yards down the field, where Todd delivered the ball on the money. Me? I had already tripped over my own feet and bellyflopped about ten yards away as Miller ran untouched for a score. I hoped that my inept footwork went unnoticed.

"Nice footwork," said Todd between obnoxious chuckles.

"Why don't you go out for the ballet team?" Milton snorted.

Well, that wasn't so bad. They were jerks anyway. What else would you expect? It's not like anyone important noticed.

"Hey, Casey," yelled out Amy from the sideline, where the cheerleaders were practicing. "We could use some of that form over here."

At least Danielle didn't . . .

"Have a nice trip?" howled Danielle. "See you next fall!"

Not very original, but it didn't make it hurt any less.

"You'll get 'em next time," cheered Nina.

And then it hit me. Not an idea. The ball. While I was thinking of how idiotic I must have looked, I ended up looking even more idiotic as the ball was thrown in my direction. Unfortunately, I was looking the wrong way.

"Nice catch," yelled Todd.

"Way to keep your head in the game," called out Milton.

At least Danielle didn't say anything. She was too busy laughing. It's amazing how much more embarrassing it is when the girl you like is laughing hysterically at you fouling up.

Then it hit me. This time it was an idea. And you'll never guess what it was.

SWOOSH!

Oh, you did guess it.

37

Another Fifteen Minutes of Practice

"**S**ince when do you wear a watch to practice?" asked Coach.

"It's not a watch. It's a football refigurator."

I just love watching Coach's face twitch.

"Um. Yeah. Okay, Little. Go in for Brosnan. No use hurting the regulars right before the big play-off game."

I ran in . . . again.

"Hey, Stacy," said the oh-so-hysterical Todd. "Ready to get pummeled?"

"Yeah? By you and what army?" I said defiantly.

"Company A," he said, pointing to his right fist, "and Company B," he said, pointing to his left. "And Company C and D," he added as he pointed to his elbows. "And Company—"

"Okay, okay. I get the idea."

I've got to remember that being overconfident can get me in a lot of trouble.

As before, I lined up on defense guarding Miller. The ball was centered as Miller zigged. But before he got to *zag,* I headed to a spot one step in front of where I knew Todd was going to throw the ball. Todd delivered the ball and Miller was right where he should have been. But before the ball reached Miller, it reached me, and I intercepted it.

The silence on the field was broken only by the disgusting sound of everyone's eyeballs popping out as they watched me run untouched into the end zone. I've got to admit that running wasn't all that difficult since no one had tried to tackle me. By the time anyone recovered from the shock of my actually catching the ball, I had scored.

"Way to go, Mr. Touchdown!" screamed Nina.

"Nice play," yelled Coach. "I didn't know you had it in you."

"You were lucky, Little," said Todd. "I underthrew that. It won't happen again."

As I walked back to my position I saw Tractor shaking his head with that little smile of his. It was hard to miss the fact that the cheerleaders, including Danielle, had seen the play too. I made sure that she didn't notice that I was noticing. It was part of being oh so cool.

On the very next play, Todd sent Miller long. I'm surprised I didn't catch a cold from the breeze Broderick created as he ran past me. But Todd made so sure he wouldn't underthrow Miller, he threw it ten yards over his head.

This one's gonna be sweet.

SWOOSH!

"Hey, Stacy," said Todd. "Ready to get pummeled?"

"Yeah? By your Company A and Company B fists?"

"Um, yeah," said the ever-so-confused Todd. "Don't you forget it."

As I had already done twice before, I lined up on defense, guarding Miller.

Again, the ball was centered as Miller zigged, zagged, etcetera. And again I intercepted the ball. I ran it into the end zone, and this time it actually felt pretty good.

"Way to go, Mr. Touchdown!" screamed Nina.

"Nice play," said Coach. "I didn't know you had it in you."

"You were lucky, Little," said Todd. "I underthrew that. It won't happen again."

I just smiled and walked back to my position, and this time I winked at Danielle. I'm pretty sure she smiled back at me.

On the next play, instead of lining up opposite Miller, I went right to the spot where I knew that Todd would overthrow the ball. Miller took off, Todd threw, and the ball went right where he had thrown it fifteen minutes before, ten yards too far and right into my arms. Another interception.

"Wow," said Coach.

"Great anticipation, Casey," complimented Miller.

"Dumb luck," said Todd.

"Lookin' good," yelled out Danielle.

Nina just raised an eyebrow.

Two plays. Two interceptions. I was hot. At least the Go-back was. Before practice was over, I had intercepted seven passes, recovered three fumbles, and just for good measure told Todd what play he would be calling next.

I walked off the field as if I had just won the championship game myself. I'm pretty sure even Tractor gave me a wink. He could have had a bug in his eye, but I'm going with the wink. Everyone was slapping me on the back. Everyone except Nina. She just walked away shaking her head. I wonder if she had any idea that I had a *little* help from the Go-back.

"C'était formidable," said Danielle.

I have no idea what she said, but from the way she said it, I guessed it was pretty good.

"Be ready to play Saturday," said Coach.

Wow. That was about the best thing I had ever heard.

"How about going out for pizza with us after the game on Saturday?" asked Danielle.

And that was the new best thing I ever heard.

Was my life becoming everything I had ever hoped for? It would take less than a day to find out.

AND the ANSWER
IS "YOU BET!"

Everything seemed pretty normal at lunch the next day. Well, except for . . .

"Would you like to sit at our table?" asked Danielle.

I was being asked to sit at the lunch table with the world's most popular kids. At least *my world's*.

"Sorry, Miss Frenchie Pants," Nina answered for me. "Casey always sits with—"

"Sure," I interrupted.

Come on. Have you ever taken a good look at Danielle? You would have done the same thing. I mean if you were a guy.

"Casey . . . ?" questioned Nina.

"It's what Grandpop would have wanted," I said.

Not sure if she was buying that.

"Jerk."

Now I was sure. She wasn't.

Next stop, Popularville. Although the mayor of Popularville wasn't going to be too happy.

"What's Wimpface doing here?" asked Todd as I reached the popular kids' table.★

"He's with me," said Danielle.

You have no idea how good that sounded.

"Have you gone brain dead, Danielle?" asked Todd.

You have no idea how bad that sounded.

"Afraid he might intercept your sandwich before you get it to your mouth?" said Amy.

Now you'd think that would make Todd angry with Amy, but he just glared harder at me. I guess just because almost everyone in school thinks you're popular, it doesn't mean that you're popular with the popular kids. It's really a lot of math.

"Just because he guessed right in practice doesn't mean he's gonna do anything but haul the water for the game," said Todd.

"You're just jealous," said Danielle. "You'll show him that you're better than he is Saturday, won't you, Case?"

I was hoping that was one of those rhetorical questions that didn't call for me to actually answer it.

"Well, Schmace," Todd said, obviously running out of crummy nicknames to call me. "You think you're better than me?"

Everyone at the table stared at me, waiting to see if I'd

★You know how in the movies it always seems that the most popular kids in school are also the biggest jerks? Well, I'm here to tell you, it's true in books, too. At least in this one.

cut my own throat. Confidently, I readied my answer.

"Um, I . . . uh, well . . . you see . . . I, um . . ."

"Looking forward to playing with you Saturday," a soft yet strong voice said.

It seemed like the world stood still. At least the winners' table stopped in mid-bite.

Without another word, Tractor moved on and left the lunchroom.

39

The Night Before
the Day After

I stood in my room, staring in the mirror, seeing not a real water boy but a real player. For the first time in my life, I was actually excited about a game. Besides it being the play-offs, a big game—the Scieszka Cheesemen versus the Pilkey Underpants Guys—my focus was on more than how much water I would spill. Tomorrow, after the game, I was going out with the most popular kids in school. While I didn't want to jump to conclusions—but in this case I will—if I was with the most popular kids in school, then therefore didn't that make me a popular kid? I think it's called contagious popularity.

I put on the Go-back, admiring how good-looking I was when I had some power over my life.

"Thanks again, Grandpop," I said, looking at

Grandpop's picture, which didn't seem as cheery as I first remembered.

CRACK!

What the . . . ?

CRACK!

The window. I opened it and—*whoosh*—a rock flew right past my head.

"Casey!"

"Nina. What do you want? And why are you throwing stones at the window instead of coming in the front door?"

"I didn't want to be seen going into a jerk's house."

"Does this have anything to do with the fact that I'm finally popular and you're not?"

"No. It has to do with you being an idiot because you think you're better than your old friends."

"That is so bogus. I don't think I'm better than my old friends. It's my new friends that are better than my old friends."

Uh-oh.

"I don't think that came out the way I meant it."

"Todd and Milton are better than Jack or Mel or Howie—or me?"

"I'm not saying that—exactly."

"You'd rather be with Amy?"

"No."

"Or Danielle?"

"Well . . . "

"So you're dropping all your old friends just to spend time with some girl who didn't give you a second thought until you played Go-back with her."

"Is that so wrong?"

"You are a stupid nitwit."

"I am not stupid. Didn't you see me ace that history test?"

She just shook her head and walked off. She was right. I was just as bad as she had said, and I felt like a jerk because of it. But I also felt good. That happens when the best-looking girl in school actually talks to you without puking. And for the first time, other kids in school were looking at me with something that resembled respect. Maybe not actual respect, but it was close enough.

40

Game Time

The stands were full and the excitement in the air was as thick as a triple-extra-cheese pizza and twice as tasty. Even Mom and Dad showed up, and they brought Kelly, who was wearing a sweatshirt she made with my name on it—misspelled on purpose. I had never let them come before, because it wasn't like they were going to see me play. But today I even got to put that black stuff under my eyes. I still don't know what it's for, but it looks so cool. It's like you got a black eye, and you didn't even have to get punched.

I was now doubly valuable to the team. Not only did the coach want me to be ready to play, but he knew I was the only one capable of handling the all-important job of keeping the squad healthy . . . and wet. I was running the water in and out like a pro water b—, I mean, manager. Not a drop spilled, and each time I ran back to the sideline, I could see Danielle and the rest of the cheerleaders rooting us on.

The teams kept going up and down the field. Almost every time Tractor touched the ball, he scored. With the Pilkeys putting four of their best linemen on Tractor, every time we scored a touchdown, they struck back with one of their own.

The hitting was hard. It seemed that after every play, someone else was being carried off the field. If this kind of bone-jarring play continued, we could run out of players. But before we would actually exhaust our player supply, the coach would definitely have to put me in. All you had to do was look at the fear on Coach's face to know that. I mean, he saw how I played at practice, but I'm sure he thought that must have been a fluke.

The game was tied going into the fourth quarter. I think Tractor had gained something like twelve hundred yards running the ball. Todd was passing pretty well too. Problem is, the Underpants Guys were just as good.

With about a minute left in the game and Pilkey with the ball, our next-to-the-last defensive back, Joey "Limp" Sacco, was carried off the field. Coach called on me to go in. I picked up the water pail and . . .

"Forget the pail, Little," said Coach. "Go in for Sacco."

Wow. My big chance. I started to go in.

"Hey, leave the watch here," yelled Coach.

Leave the Go-back? He has got to be kidding. I couldn't play worth a darn without it. But maybe this was meant to be. Maybe this was a sign that I should go in and depend on myself to be the best that I could be and everything would be all right.

Na-a-ah.

"The wristband is stuck, Coach," I mumbled as I ran onto the field. "Can't get it off. Sorry."

I got into the huddle with Todd, Milton, Tractor, and the rest of the defense.

"Just stay out of the way and don't screw up, Stacy," said my supportive teammate Todd.

The Pilkey Guys lined up, and I was pretty sure that they would run the play in my direction. I was the newest player out there, and they always test the one who's the most untested. The quarterback dropped back and looked right in my direction, the same direction in which their receiver was leaving me in the dust. He caught the ball on the dead run as the game clock counted down. That's when Tractor came out of nowhere and hit the Pilkey receiver so hard that we were all surprised the kid stayed in one piece. One thing that wasn't surprising was that he coughed up the ball.

There it was, rolling around, no one within ten yards of

where it had landed. With the speed and force of Tractor's tackle, Tractor and the receiver had rolled some fifteen yards out of bounds. I was a good twenty-five yards away, as I had forgotten which direction we were going in and ran in the opposite direction. It's a mistake anyone could make . . . if they were me.

Still, if someone on our team picked up the ball, we'd not only keep the game tied, but a clear path to the end zone was waiting.

After what seemed like . . . fifteen minutes, someone finally picked up the ball. But it wasn't a Cheeseman. It was an Underpants Guy who picked it up and, before anyone on Scieszka could react, he had scored . . . the winning touchdown.

At least it wasn't my fault. Not that much, anyway.

"Nice coverage, Little," said Todd.

"Great play," added Milton.

Look up "cynical" in the dictionary and you'll find pictures of Todd and Milton there. Look up "sucky player" and I'm pretty sure I'd be looking back at you.

Danielle just stood there shaking her head. I was already writing off the after-game pizza, along with my newfound popularity.

Unless . . . Why not?

SWOOSH!

41

score!

Once again, I was whisked back . . . back to . . .

"Forget the pail, Little," said Coach. "Go in for Sacco.

"Hey, leave the watch here," yelled Coach.

"Not on your life."

"What did you say?" growled Coach.

I didn't think I'd said it so loud.

"I said, 'There's snot on your wife.' Um, you ought to get her a tissue."

As he looked into the stands for his wife, I ran out onto the field.

I got into the huddle with Todd, Milton, Tractor, and the rest of the defense.

"Just stay out of the way," said Todd. "And don't screw up, Stacy."

"Maybe you just better stay out of my way," I said with a sneer, trying to raise one side of my upper lip to look tough. All I ended up doing was looking like I had something wrong with my mouth.

"You makin' faces at me?" growled Milton.

"An involuntary twitch. It's hereditary."

"Jerk," blared Milton.

"Yes," I agreed. "Yes, I am."

The Pilkey Guys lined up, and I knew they'd be running the play right at me. But instead of me lining up against the receiver I was supposed to defend, I went over to the part of the field where Tractor would cause the fumble.

The receiver laughed.

"Get on your man!" shouted Coach.

"Where are you going, dimwit?" yelled Todd.

It seemed like our entire side of the stands was screaming for me to move into the "right" position.

Todd tried to call a timeout, but before he could, the Pilkey quarterback took the ball, dropped back, and threw the ball right into the hands of the receiver I was supposed to be covering. He caught the ball on the dead run as the game clock counted down to 00:00. I waited where the Tractor-receiver collision was about to take place.

Tractor rolled toward the receiver. He had no idea what I knew or how bad he would feel in just a couple of seconds.

BAM!

Maybe less than a couple.

Being as close as I was, the impact was much more resounding than it had seemed the first time around. I'm guessing the vibration from the hit registered at least a six on the Richter scale. And as before, the ball popped free.

This time there was someone nearby. *Moi* (that's "me" in French).

With no one else around, the ball bounced quickly and hard. I went to grab it, but not being quite as coordinated as I'd like, I missed it as it smashed against my wrist. Luckily, I got it on the second bounce. Buoyed by the crowd, I ran past the cheerleaders, who were not exactly jumping for joy as much as giving some sort of cheer with their fists. Fists that seemed to be aimed directly at me.

From behind, instead of Pilkey players running me down, I was being chased by ten very angry teammates. That's when I realized that the cheers I was hearing were coming from the Pilkey stands because, well, because I was . . .

RUNNING IN THE WRONG DIRECTION!

But I had gained such confidence that I didn't worry a bit. I just put on the brakes and went to the old trusty Goback which . . . WASN'T THERE?

NO-O-O-O-O!

It must have been knocked loose when the ball hit it.

That meant whatever I was going to do I was going to have to do on my own. YIKES!

Depending on myself was not a thing I was very good at.

That's when the next best thing to the Go-back showed up—Tractor.

"Follow me," he whispered in my ear.

And with that Tractor turned and, like a nuclear-charged tank, began to escort me down the field, mowing down Pilkey players as if they were defenseless blades of grass. This time the cheers were coming from the Scieszka fans. The twenty, the thirty, the forty. It's pretty easy to run when you're riding a ninety-mile-per-hour plow. As the Underpants Guys flew right and left, I was pulled along by a mighty draft generated by Tractor.

As we passed the cheerleaders again, I'm pretty sure Danielle blew me a kiss. She could have been just wiping her mouth, but as fast as I was running, I couldn't be sure.

With ten Pilkey Guys strewn over the field in all sorts of mangled disarray, only one defender stood between me and the end zone; between me and the winning touchdown; between me and a lifetime of popularity. And I was going to gain this fame all on my own, without any help from the Go-back. Yessiree, no help at all. Unless, of course, you want to count the little bit of support from Tractor. All right, a ton of support from Tractor. Still, this was so great!

The last Pilkey Guy—they called him Rex, as in *Tyrannosaurus rex*—was actually bigger than Tractor, but that didn't slow down Tractor one bit. If anything, it seemed to make him even more enthusiastic about putting a hole through the guy. Or is it *in* the guy? Prepositions are a killer, aren't they?

Bam!

The vibration from their collision is still being felt throughout the school. I'm serious—if you go to a Scieszka Middle School game today, they have seat belts in the grandstand to keep you from falling out of your seat.

Tractor and Rex rolled out of bounds in a heap of middle school blob as I headed for *end zone heaven*.

The twenty-yard line, the fifteen, the ten, the five, the four, the three, the two, the one, the three-quarter, the half, the three-eighth, the three-sixteenths, the . . .

It actually didn't take that long, but when you're in the middle of something this awesome, you want it to last as long as possible. Finally—

SCORE!

Scieszka wins! Scieszka wins!

The stands emptied out and before you could say (actually, you wouldn't have time to say anything, so why even try?), I was up on the shoulders of millions of fans. Okay, not millions, but you get the idea. They circled the field with me on their shoulders. Boy, being popular can really make you dizzy. The fans were in such a frenzy that when I fell off their shoulders on the thirtieth time around the field, they kept on going around the field five more times before they noticed I wasn't up there anymore.

The cheerleaders made up a cheer.

"Two-four-six-eight, Casey's play was really great! Eight-six-four-two, Casey's quite attractive, too."[*]

"Yay, Casey!" yelled Danielle. "Remember the victory party!"

Like I would ever forget.

Can you believe it? Even Todd was happy for me.

"You were just lucky to be in the right place at the right time," said Todd, smirking.

Smirking was about as close as he ever got to being happy.

I looked for Nina and the guys, but they were nowhere in sight. It would have been nice to share this with them. And where was Tractor? To be honest, he had more to do with the win than the Go-back or I did. That's when I heard the siren.

I ran over and saw something I'll never forget. What was it again? Oh yeah, right. The indestructible Tractor Thinthith had been destructed. Tractor's leg was twisted in a shape that more resembled a pretzel than a leg. Maybe he was clenching his teeth a little bit more than normal, but with all the pain that he had to be feeling, you wouldn't

---

[*]Okay, I made up the part about the cheer, but if you want you can use it at your own school's games.

know it from his face. If it was me, I wouldn't be yelling out in agony either. That's because I would have already passed out from the pain.

Was it my fault that Tractor got hurt? It was his choice to do the blocking, right? Who was I kidding? It was my fault, darn it. The attendants lifted Tractor into the ambulance and closed the doors.

Ah, Tractor was a tough guy. He'd heal before you knew it.

"I never saw a leg twisted up like that," said the attendant. "Makes me hungry for a pretzel."

"Will he be okay next week for the championship game?" I asked.

"Next week?" the attendant said, shaking his head. "He'll be lucky if he ever walks again."

Gulp. Double gulp.

"Is this yours?"

It was Nina, standing there with the Go-back.

"Where did you find it?

"Right where you picked up the fumble—the first, second, third, or whatever time."

Hmm-m-m. She didn't seem all that happy about us winning.

I took the Go-back and put it on.

"Um. Did you use it while you had it?" I asked.

"Why? I already know what a jerk you are. Why would

I want to see that more than once?"

"Nina . . . ?"

"What?"

I knew it might have seemed like I was rejecting my old friends. I should explain to her why it's so important for me to sit with the popular kids. That's what a guy with real nerve would do.

"Never mind," I said nervelessly.

"Enjoy pizza with your *friends*."

She said the word "friends" in a way that you could pretty much figure out she didn't think they were really friends. She began to walk away.

"Hey," I called out. "How about you coming with me to the victory party?"

"My old friends are fine, thank you."

And she was gone. So was the ambulance. My mind was going crazy. How can I feel so lousy when I should be on top of the world?

I had to push through a whole bunch of people patting me on the back to get to the locker room.

"You surprised the heck out of me, Little," said Coach. "Make sure you're ready for the championship game next week."

"Yeah. With Tractor out, we'll need everyone who can strap on a jock," said Milton.

Todd slammed Milton across the top of his head.

"It was just plain luck," said Todd. "He was in the right place at the right time. Dumb luck. Can't say the same for Tractor."

Yeah. Can't say anything for Tractor. He hardly said anything for himself. What a bad break. I wished I could . . . Wait a minute. I checked the Go-back and there was just about enough time.

"Little for President!" one of the players yelled.

I was afraid my political career would have to wait.

I pressed the Go-back and . . .

SWOOSH!

42

Here we Go Again

Once again I was staring straight at Tractor's butt as he chewed up the Pilkey Guys in front of him. I wasn't sure what I was going to do, but I knew I had to do something. We (pretty much really just Tractor) were bearing down fast on *Tyrannosaurus rex*.

"Tractor!" I yelled. "Over here! Watch out!"

"Huh?"

Running as fast as he was and turning to look back at me, he was easily pushed aside by Rex.

I took off running as fast as I could toward the center of the field. Unfortunately, Rex was running the same way. If I could muster up all the strength I had, perhaps I could outrun—

KER-RASH!

Now a lot of you might say that before I was obliterated by Rex, I should have just used the Go-back. After all, I already knew where the Go-back was and all I had to do was pick it up and go back to make things right—and still score.

Sounds good, huh? Except for one little matter. *Tyrannosaurus rex* hit me so hard, he knocked me out cold. Actually, I could have been out *warm,* but being that I was unconscious, I wouldn't really know.

"Huh. What the hey?"

Do you know how bad smelling salts smell? Whew! Who could stay passed out when they're sticking that stuff up your nose?

"How ya doin', son?" asked the paramedic.

"Okay, I guess." I figured the humongous headache didn't really count.

"Are you sure, honey?" asked Mom.

"Couldn't be better," I assured her, knowing if I didn't say that I'd end up in bed for a week.

"Nice try, son," said Dad.

"Yeah," added Kelly. "If you tried any harder, we would have lost."

"Thanks, Dad," I said, ignoring Kelly. "Wish I could have scored and broken the tie."

"The tie was broken," corrected Dad. "You fumbled and—"

"Oh no. We lost the game?"

"Not with me on the field," said Todd pompously. "Thanks to you being your normal clod self, I am once again the hero . . . as usual."

"Picked up the ball and scored," added Todd's dad, who never missed a game.

"Is my boy something, or what?" he added.

I never knew exactly what that meant, "something, or what." I guess it's supposed to be something good, but it's hard to understand why being "something, or what" is so hot. Still, I wish my dad could have felt that way about me.

"You'll get them next time, son," said Dad.

Okay, maybe he did feel that way about me. I guess Dad wasn't disappointed in me, but I also realized that not only wasn't I the hero, I could have been the . . .

"Nah-h-h-h," nahh'ed Milton as he passed by.

. . . goat.

"Are you okay, Casey?"

Omigod. It was Danielle and, even though I was entirely responsible for almost losing the game, she was still concerned about my health.

"I'm fine."

"Great," she said.

"I really appreciate that you—"

Smack!

She slapped me right across the face.

"That's for lying to me that your family is French."

I looked at Mom and Dad, who gave me one of those "Hey, if you're going to lie to people and you want us to back it up, then you better fill us in first" looks.

Then they immediately followed that with another look that meant "Actually, even if you had told us, we still would have told the truth, because there is no way that we would condone your lying."

"I said 'was' French. You know, before the family's big French-to-American conversion, which erased all memory of former nationalities."

No one was buying it. Would you?

"Are we still on for pizza?" I asked Danielle.

"In your dreams."

How did she know about last night?

SLAP!

"That's for putting me in your dream last night," said Danielle as she walked off in a huff.

I started to get up.

"Hold on, kid. Got to check you out first," the paramedic said. "You've been down for over fifteen minutes."

"Fifteen?"

"Could be sixteen. How are you feeling?"

"I was feeling pretty good until now. Can I go?"

"Was he unconscious?" asked Dad.

"Actually," explained the paramedic, "the boy just had a

classic case of not paying attention, or what we in the medical profession call NPA. Very common in mid-grade. Your son's case is just a tad more . . . intense."

"Is this yours?"

It was Nina, standing there with the Go-back. Jack, Howie, and Mel stood behind her.

"How many times did you use it before you lost it?"

I took the Go-back and slid it on.

"Nina . . . ?"

"What?"

"Nothin', I guess."

"Enjoy pizza with your *friends*," she said as she started to walk off with the guys.

"Um . . . Nina."

"What?"

"Have you seen Tractor?"

"Why? You want to ream him out for not carrying you into the end zone?"

"Is he okay?"

"After that last play, he kind of limped off the field," said Jack.

"Yeah, it was really weird," said Howie. "He was blocking every player that came near you. Then, for some reason, he turned away from that last big guy and looked back at you. He probably twisted his ankle then."

"Funny," said Mel. "I've seen every game that Tractor's

played, but I never saw him back off from hitting anyone."

"I guess even Tractor can be afraid," said Jack.

"Yeah, it's weird," I said, knowing that being scared had nothing to do with him turning away—or twisting his ankle, for that matter.

How could I ever explain to these guys what really happened?

"Yeah," Nina chimed in with a smirk. "It's really weird."

Just a guess here, but I think the only thing that Nina thought was weird was the mess that the Go-back and I had gotten into. Actually, it was way more my fault than the Go-back's.

"So, why aren't you getting ready to have pizza with *Danielle*?" asked Nina.

She said "Danielle" the way she said "friends" before.

"Ah. I think I'm gonna take a pass."

"Well," she said. "If you want to go out with friends who may not be all that popular, you're welcome to come with us."

"Thanks, but I'm not really hungry."

"Not hungry?" said Mom. "Maybe you should go to the hospital."

"Your loss," said Nina as she and the guys walked away.

"Casey," said Mom. "You better go and change out of your uniform. This is late for Kelly."

"Thanks, Mom," Kelly said with a sneer. "Why don't you just tell everyone I wear diapers."

"Um. Y'know, Mom, maybe I will take Nina up on that pizza."

"Just make sure you don't come home too late," said Dad.

"And not too much pizza," said Mom. "You know you get gassy."

No one need worry about that. I wasn't going to have any pizza.

43

Entering the Not-a-Victory-party Neighborhood

Did you ever find yourself in a neighborhood that you've never been in before, a neighborhood that was so different from yours that it totally freaked you out? No? Thanks a lot. Now I really feel like a wimp.

I was pretty sure this was where Tractor lived. I had only been there on one Halloween night. I didn't go there to trick or treat, though. I went because everyone said that Tractor's house was as close to a real **HAUNTED** house as you would ever see outside of Disneyland. I don't know if it was really **HAUNTED**, but if it wasn't, it should have been. How **SCARY** was it? As I drew closer to his house, **THUNDER ROARED AND LIGHTNING FLASHED.*** I held one finger on the Go-back just in case I had to make a fast getaway.

---

*Okay, I made up the **THUNDER AND LIGHTNING** part for effect, but still, it was pretty spooky.

I don't know exactly why I went to see Tractor. There was just something inside me that was telling me to. I was half hoping he wouldn't be there. Actually the *hoping he wouldn't be there* percentage was closer to 99 percent.

Unfortunately—big unfortunately—Tractor was sitting on the porch. He looked at me like I was the last person on Earth he expected to see. Coincidentally, I was the last person on Earth that I'd expect to see there too.

He had a large bandage on his forehead, a huge shiner under his right eye, and a big old ice bag tied around his knee with a rope. A pair of crutches leaned against the wall.

"You look pretty banged up," I said.

"Nah." He smiled. "I put this stuff on just to look cool."

"Good game, huh?" I said.

Tractor shook his head no.

"Yeah, I didn't think so either," I said.

I stood there swinging my arms back and forth as nothing was said for what seemed like an hour.

"Well, as long as you're okay, I guess I'll head over to—"

Just as I was leaving, the door swung open. That's when I heard the **MENACING** sound of **CREAKING** wheels. A wheelchair rolled out carrying the oldest lady I've ever seen. She had to be well over sixty. Maybe even sixty-two.

"Oh, I see you have company, Norman," said his grand-mother.

I had never heard anyone call Tractor Norman. But I guess since she was his grandmother, it's a pretty safe bet he'd let her get away with it.

"Can I get you something to drink?" she asked me.

"No thank you, ma'am. I really can't stay. Some other time."

"But what if you're not thirsty then?" she replied.

I had no idea how to answer that, but it didn't matter because before I could say a word, she had already gone back into the house. I'm pretty sure I heard her laughing inside.

"My grandmother thinks she's a comedian."

Wow. Tractor actually said something—to me.

"She's been looking out for me ever since I **KILLED** my parents."

"Uh-h-h-h-h-h" was the only sound that escaped from my mouth.

That's when Tractor, the guy who I only saw smile once before, let out the biggest laugh I ever heard.

"And then I **MURDERED** the detectives who tried to arrest me."

His laugh boomed even louder and so contagiously that I couldn't help but laugh, too. Then, as quickly as he started to laugh, he stopped and growled, "What's so funny?"

"Um, I, uh, just thought, that, you know, with you laughing, that you were kind of joking about—I mean, I'm sorry if . . . "

That's when he laughed even harder than before. I stood there not knowing if he was joking or if he was joking about joking. I mean, could I laugh or not? It was like being at the dinner table and you and your sister or brother want to burst out laughing about something but you know if you do, your mom will pop you one. It isn't easy being a kid. It's even harder being me.

Tractor stopped laughing. His face seemed a whole lot more relaxed than I ever remembered seeing.

"My parents died when I was about two. I hardly remember them."

And then I saw something that I never thought I would see: a tear. A tear that slowly fell down Tractor's cheek. He brushed it away, hoping that I didn't see it.

For what seemed like forever, we both just stood there (well, he was sitting) and kind of nodded. Tractor finally broke the nodding cycle.

"But I'm pretty sure I didn't **MURDER** them."

This time no tears or laughter. Instead, an easy smile appeared on his face.

"Sorry I blew that last block," said Tractor.

"You didn't blow it. I was the one who screwed up. In fact, you actually did blow *Tyrannosaurus rex* away with one of the most awesome blocks I've ever seen."

"What are you talking about?"

"It's really hard to explain. In fact, it's impossible. You just have to believe me, the only one at fault for the fumble was me."

"Yeah, okay."

To this day I don't think he ever believed me.

"I'm thinking of getting some pizza. Wanna come?"

"Aren't you afraid I might **MURDER** you?"

"Uh . . . "

"I'm kidding. I think I'll pass. I really don't like hanging out. Besides, I gotta help my grandma."

He got up kind of shaky.

"Okay. Well, hope you feel better."

He just nodded and, with the help of his crutches, walked to the door.

"I meant what I said about the game. It was me that screwed up, not you."

I don't know if he heard me as he walked into the house, but I think I said it as much for me as I did for him.

44

The Victory Party

I opened the door of Dom's Three Pizzas for the Price of One and a Half. Anyone else would have named it Dom's Two Pizzas for the Price of One, but Dom was so proud of his flair for math he couldn't help but let everyone know. He even sliced his pizzas into nine slices instead of eight because he wanted to prove that mathematically, it could be done. I actually think he did that to make the pizzas tough to split up. Of course, if you were a party of three, you had it made.

Dom's was crowded, and everyone was in a pretty good mood. However, as soon as I walked in, the mood became even—gooder. Why not? I was a fun target.

"Hey, look," yelled out Milton. "It's Mr. Fumble."

"Stacy" didn't sound so bad anymore. I was guessing

that chances of being invited over to the popular table were dropping fast. Thankfully, Nina and the guys were still there.

"Mind if I sit with you guys?" I asked.

"If you don't mind sitting with a bunch of losers," said Nina, who was getting really good at sarcasm. That's when I noticed that Howie, Jack, and Mel were soaked. I looked over at Todd, who shot me a wink. One of those winks that said, "You're next."

"I wouldn't want to sit anywhere else," I said as I sat down. "Hey, guys, how much longer are we going to take this?"

"I guess until we graduate," said Jack.

"Yeah," agreed Howie. "If those guys let us live that long."

"It's just not fair," I said as if "fair" had anything to do with how life worked.

"Any ideas?" asked Nina.

"Yeah. Any ideas, loser?"

Ah, the charms of Todd.

"And in case you didn't get my meaning, I meant *l-o-s-e-r*."

"Wow, Todd," I foolishly said. "You can spell. What's next? Wiping yourself?"

Okay. That was pretty disgusting. But so was Todd.

Dom's stopped cold. Todd glared. It was like I had

slapped him across the face—with a dirty diaper.

"What did you say?" he fumed.

I thought it was better not to make things worse.

"Nothing."

"He said, 'When are you going to learn how to wipe yourself?'" Nina *helped*.

Obviously, Nina thought that my life was not worth living.

"Is she right, loser?" asked Todd.

"I only meant it as a question, not necessarily a statement of fact."

I don't think that satisfied Todd, as he lifted me by my collar and out of my seat. My life passed before my eyes. To be honest, a lot of different lives passed before my eyes. It kind of distracted me from what I figured was going to be a not very pleasant next few minutes.

I didn't think I could wait any longer. I reached for the Go-back.

"What do you think you're doing?" asked Todd as he let go of my collar, grabbing onto my wrist, just as I pushed the Go-back.

SWOOSH!

45

Todd Joins the club

I again found myself walking to Dom's, and while I was well aware that it might be better to leave things the way they were and just skip Dom's, I thought there must be something I could do to make things better.

I entered Dom's and rewatched the reaction to my arrival.

"Hey, look," yelled out Milton. "It's Mr. Fumble."

Everyone laughed. Everyone but Todd. He just sat there with the oddest look on his face. As I walked over to Nina and the guys, he jumped up, grabbed me, and pulled me into the men's room. Seems like that's where he does all his business.

"What the heck happened, Little?" he said as he shoved me against the wall.

"I have no idea what you're talking about." I really didn't.

"Don't be smart. You know what I mean. I was talking to you, and then all of a sudden I'm back at my table and everybody's repeating what they said before. What happened?"

Oh no. Somehow when I went back, so did Todd. I quickly covered up the Go-back. Not quickly enough. Todd pulled my hand away and grabbed my wrist. I tried to stop him, but he pulled off the Go-back.

"What's this?"

"A watch. What do you think it is?"

"I never saw a watch like this."

"It was my grandfather's. It's old."

"How could I be standing in one place with you and the next second I'm someplace else sitting with people who were saying the same things they said before?"

"They probably had nothing else to say? You got to admit Milton's pretty repetitious."

"Very funny. It wasn't only Milton. It was everyone. I felt like I was saying stuff I thought I said fifteen minutes ago. Even the pizza that I was in the middle of eating was gone."

"You probably forgot that you finished it."

"Then why did the waitress bring it over again?"

"Great service?"

"The dirty napkins were clean."

"I've always thought of you as extremely neat."

"Stop jerking me around, Little. I had my hands on you and then, all of a sudden, you're not even there anymore."

"Have you ever heard of déjà vu?"

"It's some kind of French cheese, right?"

"Um. Sure. But it also means that things that have never happened seem like they have."

"You mean like science fiction?"

"Haven't you ever been someplace and it seems like you were there before?"

"Yeah. But I never thought I ate a pizza and fifteen minutes later found out I didn't."

"That's kind of Italian déjà vu."

"Don't mess with my mind, Little."

What about messing with my mind? The entire time he was talking, all I was thinking was *Please don't press the Go-back*. If he did, he's the only one who would go back. Then the last fifteen minutes would disappear, and I'd have no idea what had happened.

"Could I have my watch back, please? It holds a lot of sentimental value."

"You know what? I think I'm gonna keep it for a while, just to make sure you don't try anything funny."

Uh-oh.

"Funny? I won't be doing anything funny. I've sworn

off comedy. There's way too much humor in this world, if you ask me. In fact, I've even sworn off laughing. Who needs laugh lines at my age?"

"Well, I'm keeping it anyway. And if you tell anyone, including your parents, I'm gonna be looking for you, and it won't be just for a toilet dunk."

Gulp.

"In fact, just because you're an idiot . . ."

46

He Meant It

"**M**ind if I sit with you guys?" I asked with my head freshly flushed.

"If you don't mind sitting with a bunch of losers," said Nina.

"Looks like you still fit in," said the similarly soaked Howie.

"I wouldn't want to sit anywhere else," I said, and I meant it. "Hey, guys, how much longer are we going to take this?"

"I guess until we graduate," said Jack.

"If we don't drown by then," added Mel.

"I mean it, guys. If we let Todd, Milton, and the rest of those clowns keep doing what they're doing to us and we keep taking it, we can only blame ourselves."

"So what do we do," said Jack. "Punch 'em out?"

"Yeah," said Mel. "You have a plan?"

I nodded with a knowing smile, even though I knew nothing. Worse, I didn't have the Go-back to help.

Even worse—Todd did.

47

MaN, I DiDn't
see THis coming

Important Notice!

This is really weird and I'm not sure how to explain it, but I'm afraid, because of the circumstances, I'm going to have to take a little break here. You see, after Todd got hold of the Go-back, there were certain things that happened, then didn't happen, then happened, then didn't happen again, of which I have no recollection. I mean, it was now Todd going back and erasing stuff, so he's the only one who knows what happened that doesn't even exist anymore.

So, unfortunately, I am forced to turn over this part of the book to Todd. It's not something I want to do, but I have no choice. I will be back, I hope.

Just do me a favor—after Todd's part is finished, please let me know what he did. I figure there might be a lot of garbage I'm going to have to clean up.

Later,

Casey

#

todd Here

Hey, how ya doin'? I'm Todd. I might be one of the coolest kids at Jon Scieszka Middle School, if not the coolest. In fact, I'm sure I am. I've never narrated a book before, so bear with me. Anyway, here goes.

Best,

Todd

I went back to my table, the one with the most popular kids in school, because, of course, I am one. Seeing Jerkface squish back to the losers' table, Milton and the guys high-five'd me.

"Where'd you get that piece of junk?" asked Milton about the piece of junk I got from Little.

"The twerp kept screwing around with it. I figured it

would be safer with me. I just don't trust that little creep."

"Let me see it," said Danielle as she pulled it away. "Wow. It's really old. What's this on the other side? 'Push this to go back in time.'"

"Let me see that," I said as I grabbed it back from her.

Yeah, right. Like you could go back in time just by pushing this . . .

SWOOSH!

49

what the . . . ?

"Hey, look," yelled out Milton. "It's Mr. Fumble."

"How many times are you going to say that?" I asked, 'cause he did say it a few pages ago, didn't he?

"What are you talking about, Todd?" exclaimed Milton. "I only said it once—when Little just walked in."

That was almost fifteen minutes ago and . . .

"Hey, where's Little's watch?" I asked.

"You mean the one he's wearing?" asked Amy.

She was right. Little was wearing his watch. The watch I had—I mean, I *thought* I had on.

"Um, guys. Wasn't I just wearing that watch?"

"Right," said Danielle. "How hard did you get hit on the head during the game?"

Little was staring at me really weird.

"What are you looking at, Loser?" I asked.

"Nothing," said Little as he walked over to the jerks at the losers' table.

Something was wrong or weird. Maybe even both. I jumped up, grabbed Little, and pulled him into my "office," which some kids call the bathroom. I shoved the twerp up against the wall, feeling like I had done it before. Like déjà vu. Déjà vu? I had never even said the words "déjà vu" to myself before. At least, I thought I hadn't. What the heck was going on?

"What's going on, Little?"

"I have no idea what you're talking about."

"Don't be a wise guy. You know what I mean. I was sitting at my table with your watch on, and then when I pushed the button on the back, the watch ends up back on your wrist."

"You had my watch? Um, I mean—what watch?"

Little covered his watch like I wouldn't notice. I grabbed his wrist and pulled it off. Not the wrist, the watch.

"Come on, don't take it," he begged. "It was my grandfather's."

"I know it's your grandfather's. You already told me it was your grandfather's."

"I did? When?"

"Before. And now everything seems like it's happening again."

"Uh-oh. Um, could I have my watch back, please? It holds a lot of—"

"Sentimental value. Yeah, I know all about it. You know what? I think I'm gonna keep it for a while, just to make sure you don't try anything funny—again."

"Funny? I won't be doing anything funny. I've sworn off comedy. There's way too much humor in this world, if you ask me. In fact, I've even sworn off laughing. Who needs laugh lines at my age?"

"Shut up, shut up, shut up! I'm keeping it. And if you don't already know, you tell anyone, including your parents, I'm gonna be looking for you, and it won't be just for a toilet dunk. In fact, just because you're an idiot . . ."

I'll tell ya, there ain't nuthin' better to brighten up your day than a good old humiliating dweeb toilet dunk. It never fails to tickle the old funny bone, although I have no idea which bone that is.

I went back to my table, the one with the most popular kids in school, because, of course, I am one. Seeing Jerkface squish back to the losers' table, Milton and the guys high-five'd me.

"Where'd you get that piece of junk?" asked Milton.

"The twerp kept screwing around with it. I figured it would be safer with me. I just don't trust that little creep."

"Let me see it," said Danielle as she pulled it away. "Wow. It's really old. What's this on the other side? 'Push this to go back in time.'"

"Let me see that," I said as I grabbed it back from her.

Did all this stuff really happen before, or did I just think it did? I mean, if it all happened before, that meant that I—I feel like an idiot saying this, but that would mean I went back in time. Of course, that would be ridiculous.

"Why are you looking so weird?" asked Milton. "You look like you're trying to think of an answer to one of those questions that doesn't have an answer."

"Do you ever feel like everything that's happening now has already happened?" I asked.

"You mean like sitting here eating pizza?" asked Danielle.

"No, everything. Eating pizza, dunking the losers . . ."

"You do those things all the time," said Amy.

"I mean everything that *just* happened. Like Little walking through the door."

"Casey's not here, Todd," said Danielle. "I'm pretty sure he went home from the game with his mom and dad."

That's when Little walked in—again.

I'll skip what happened next, because you already know pretty much what kept happening. In fact, just to make sure that it was really a going-back-in-time thing, I kept going back, over and over. When I finally realized that I was really going back in time, I started to think of the amazing things that I could do. Like, every time I went back to the table I would eat all the pizza I could as fast as

I wanted. Then when I was full, I could push the button on the time-machine thingy, go back to before I ate the pizza, and get hungry all over again. That way I'd get to eat as much as I wanted. Well, it worked. I must have had fifty pizzas, although I actually only ate one. There was only one tiny little problem. I went back one more time and everything went fine, but when I pinned el Creepo to the wall, I guess I was getting a little tired from eating all that pizza, because this time when I took his watch, I dropped it. Little fell to the floor, picked up the watch, and then— oh no—he pushed the . . .

50

Todd's No Longer in the Club and, in Fact, Now He Was Never in It

. . . button.

SWOOSH!

Casey here. That was close. I had grabbed the Go-back before Todd had a chance to do any damage. I pushed the button going back to when I was first walking to Dom's. Who knows what could have happened if that big jerk had ever gotten hold of the Go-back? I figured it might be best if this time I took a pass on the pizza.

Next week's game would be for all the marbles, and I mean that literally. Don't know why, but whichever team won the championship would receive an old can filled with a thousand marbles. It was a tradition. A stupid tradition, but a tradition all the same. And this was All the Marbles Week.

That last game took a lot out of me, and with Tractor missing for the championship, I might be getting another chance to play. I went straight home. I needed the rest.

51

the storm
before the storm

There was an air of championship game excitement that swept over the school. Unfortunately, there was also an air of championship game dread. And as everyone knows, when excited air hits dreaded air, there's sure to be one heck of a storm.

Even though we were in the championship game, we were missing our best player. Maybe the best player in the whole state. Even worse, Todd seemed crankier than normal—not that he was really ever normal.

"Hey, Fumbelina," said Todd. "Gonna try to lose this week's game too?"

It's so pleasant when Todd and his mutant buddies visit our lunch table.

"Todd," I said. "Can I ask you a question?"

I could sense everyone at the table just pleading for me not to ask anything that would get them in trouble, or worse, dunked.

"Yeah. Like what?"

"Like what did we ever do to you? I mean, what are you so angry about?"

I know that was two questions, but I was the only one counting. Everyone else was just staring at us, watching the steam build in Todd's head. You could actually see the smoke beginning to billow from his ears.

Todd banged his fist on the table so hard that every tray went flying. I've never seen him get so angry. Even Milton looked nervous, which made him look even dumber.

"Don't—you—ever—ask—me—another—question . . . ever! Do you understand?"

I nodded just in case my answer would have in some way been taken as a question.

And then he just walked away, forgetting that he hadn't even tortured us in the last fifteen minutes.

"Gee," said Nina. "Todd seems to be in a better mood than usual."

"I think hating us energizes him," theorized Howie.

"And without Tractor playing, he can use all the energy he can get for Saturday's game," added Jack.

"So, in effect," said Mel, "we play an important part in helping the team win."

"Yeah," said Howie. "We ought to wear signs that say, 'We Get Dunked for Scieszka!'"

"Do we have any chance of winning?" asked Jack.

"You're all forgetting that we still have Casey," said Nina.

Every one of their faces seemed about to explode from holding back their laughs.

"You guys can laugh if you want to . . . ," I said.

"Thanks, Case," they said together.

And then they laughed—a lot.

"Don't be surprised if I end up playing an important part in winning the game."

"Why?" asked Jack. "Is Petercuskie going to make you stay on the sideline?"

Again the laughter was deafening.

"Thanks for the support, guys."

Yeah. Even my friends had their doubts. Actually, they had no doubts. They were sure I wouldn't succeed. But it wasn't my friends, or even the Go-back, that would determine whether I did or didn't do well. This time it would be me.

Coach Petercuskie worked us as hard as he ever did the entire week, and with everything that had happened I figured it might be best if I didn't bring the Go-back; I should do everything in my power—*my* power alone—to be the best I could be. It was a long shot, but maybe if I trusted in myself and my ability, I would play well. Remember, I said it was a long shot.

We practiced as hard as we could, even though, without Tractor playing, the team seemed a little less sure of winning. We would be facing the undefeated Unfortunate Eventers of Lemony Snicket Middle School. The game would be our toughest of the year. It would have been that way even if Tractor was playing.

"Hey, Little," said Coach. "I wouldn't let your fumble last week bother you . . ."

What a man. He knew how to inspire his players even if it was a player who made what could have become a game-losing fumble. That's why he was the coach.

". . . because if we're lucky, I won't have to put you in."

And that's why I was a player. And not a very good one at that. Even so, that wouldn't stop me from trying.

52

Game time!

Game day was here. I was as ready as I would ever be. Jon Scieszka Kraft Smelly Cheese Memorial Stadium was standing room only. Actually it was always standing room only as we were only a middle school and there were no seats. Just stands.

It would have been nice to have Tractor on the sideline, you know, just as an inspiration, but he hadn't shown up in school all week. Kids were saying that he was so angry that he hurt his foot that he actually chewed it off and wouldn't come back to school until a new leg grew back. I figured it was more that he was embarrassed that he wasn't indestructible.

Whether I was going to play or not, I was ready. Just to make sure I wasn't tempted to use the Go-back to cover my mistakes, I let Nina hold on to it. I trusted her more than I trusted myself, and I was pretty sure she wouldn't use it selfishly.

"Good luck," yelled Nina, who was flashing the biggest smile. She was standing with the two best-looking guys in school, who had never before given her a second look. "Isn't everything just as perfect as it could be?"

Hopefully she wasn't using it *too* selfishly.

Just like the game with Pilkey, this one would be an epic back-and-forth, give-and-take war. As the fourth quarter counted down, the score was 80–79, in favor of the Eventers. Todd had been amazing. Without Tractor there, he had definitely stepped up his game. Every pass was on target. Every time he ran, he seemed to score. Now remember, I couldn't stand the guy, so when I say he was great, he had to be pretty darn good.

I had actually gotten into the game a few times. Five, if you count the three times I carried in water. I hadn't made any mistakes, though I think that was because Todd kept the ball out of my hands. Still, it was okay. I was part of the team.

With time for only one more play in the game, Coach called for Tracy Piddle, our best receiver, to go in. But with the noise from the crowd and Piddle paying more attention to the cheerleaders than to the game, you could understand how I thought he wanted me to go in.

I couldn't say that Todd was thrilled to see me come into the huddle. In fact, he was pretty darn upset, but we had run out of time-outs so he had to go with what he had. Todd called for a running play for himself. The ball was snapped to Todd, who faked a pass to me (as if anyone really thought he would throw it my way), tucked the ball under his arm, and took off for the end zone. And he would have made it if it weren't for the fact that I ended up getting in his way. He was so busy trying not to trip over me he didn't notice the Snicket Neanderthal steam rolling straight for him.

With the game clock reading 00:00 and only one yard from the end zone, Todd was hit with such velocity and force that I was surprised he didn't lose his head. Too bad I couldn't say the same for the ball.

FUM-BLE!

As a wailing moan filled the Scieszka stands, the ball flew up in the air and toward the Snicket defensive back. The ball and defeat closed in. I jumped as I never had before and—this is going to be difficult to believe—I picked off the ball. That's right. I had caught it a yard from the goal line and, with the fear of getting severely damaged by the Neanderthal as motivation, I stepped into the end zone just as the gun went off.

Victory! And I was the hero. Me, alone, no Go-back.

The delirious crowd erupted, flooding the field. What

157

a feeling. Even Danielle and Milton were cheering for me. It might have just been the excitement of the moment, but even though Tractor wasn't there, I could almost feel him give me a thumbs-up. To top it off, and this is gonna sound pretty rotten, the best part was that Todd was miserable. I know it's not very nice to feel—oh heck, with all the grief he gave me and my friends, he deserved it. It all felt so great! I had finally understood the real lesson of the Go-back.

Do it on your own!

I got down on the ground and Nina ran up to me, jumping up and down.

"You did it! You did it!"

"Yes, I did."

"Um. I know I still have the Go-back, but you didn't somehow sneak it away from me and use it to win the game, did you?"

"Come on, Nin. It's me. Casey."

"Yes. I know. That's why I'm asking."

"No, I did not use the Go-back. I did it all on my own."

"I knew it. I knew it."

And then she did something that I kind of hoped no one else saw.

"Nina hugged Casey. Nina hugged Casey," singsonged Howie.

Too late.

"What, Howie?" asked Nina. "Are you eight years old?"

You know what, though? It wasn't that bad.

"You want to go for pizza?" asked a giddy Danielle.

I didn't have to think twice.

"You bet . . ."

Nina and the guys' faces scrunched up.

". . . but not with you."

And as Danielle's mouth dropped, their faces lit up again.

"I'm going to get out of this uniform and then let's get something to eat," I said to my *old* friends.

Running through swarms of congratulating hands pounding on my back, I headed for the locker room. The feeling was indescribable. I don't know if my cleats ever touched the ground.

53

Winning Isn't Everything. Sometimes It Isn't Anything at All

I t was just before I got to the locker room that I heard the racket.

"You make me sick!"

Pretty scary. Some old guy was screaming at someone in the parking lot.

"I did everything for you and you thank me by making me look like a fool."

Wow. I don't think I ever heard anyone get that mad. I snuck behind the bushes next to the parking lot and saw an incredible sight. The man was Todd's dad, and the guy he was screaming at was Todd.

"But Dad. We won."

"Maybe the team won, but you didn't win anything.

You fumbled the ball. If it wasn't for that little jerk lucking into getting the ball, the team would have lost."

Jerk? Lucking into getting the ball? That was raw talent.

"Dad. I got hit hard."

"I taught you to hold on to the ball. You let everyone down. You let me down."

Todd just stood there, taking it in. And I couldn't be sure, but I think he was crying. That's when his dad really blew a gasket.

"What's the matter, being a loser isn't bad enough? Now you gotta be a crybaby, too?" For the first time, Todd didn't look like a tough bully.

"Stop crying! No son of mine cries. Stop crying, I said!"

And that's when his father raised his hand as if he were going to whomp him. Todd lifted his arm to block him and his dad stopped in mid-slap.

"Ah, you make me want to puke. Find your own way home."

Mr. Dornan got into his car and, with tires screeching, wheeled out of the lot.

I didn't know what to do. I was the last person Todd would want help from. I'm sure he was already embarrassed enough. Geez, last game of the season and he was going to have to spend the rest of the year dealing with that.

I can't believe I really felt bad for Todd. Maybe this is how the world works. You're crummy to people, then other people are crummy to you. So Todd was getting back what he had given out. Right? It's like the golden rule in reverse.

As I reached the hallway just outside the locker room, I remembered something I really didn't want to remember right at that moment.

The doin' is in doin' for others or you ain't doin' nothin' at all.

Man. Even when I didn't use the Go-back, I was finding myself *going back*.

I walked outside and caught a glimpse of Todd sitting in the parking lot, just staring.

Well, I guess I gotta do what I gotta do—and I better get to doin' it fast.

54

It was Nice
for a while

I ran back to the field and found Nina and the guys.

"You're still in your uniform?" said Nina.

"Maybe he wants to make sure everyone at Dom's knows he's on the team." Mel chuckled.

I pulled Nina to the side.

"I'm sorry," she said. "But no more hugs."

"Give me the Go-back."

"What do you need it for? You won the game. What else do you want?"

"I don't have time to explain, just let me have it."

"You told me not to give it to you no matter what."

"I'm sorry I have to do this, but it's not like you're going to remember anyway."

"Huh?"

Pushing her to the ground, I pulled the Go-back off her wrist.

"Hey!" she protested.

"You know, you look pretty good today."

"Really?"

"Really."

And I pushed the Go-back.

SWOOSH!

I was just in time to run into the huddle for the last play of the game.

"Todd," I said. "Watch out for that big guy near the goal line."

"Hey, punk. Don't go telling me what to do."

The ball was snapped to Todd, he faked a pass to me, tucked the ball under his arm, and took off for the end zone. The Snicket Neanderthal headed in Todd's direction.

"Watch out!" I yelled.

All he watched was me and *bam!*

FUM-BLE! Again.

The ball flew up in the air and toward the Snicket defensive back. As the ball and defeat closed in, I jumped as I never had before—well, once before—picked off the ball, and landed on the one-yard line. But instead of running—and boy am I gonna hate myself in the morning—this time I just stood there.

Everyone started yelling, "Run, Little!" Even Todd

yelled for me to run.

Still, I stood my ground as the Neanderthal bore down on me. This wasn't going to be pretty. I gritted my teeth, figuring that in a brief moment I wouldn't have any of them left. A split second before I was going to be (gulp) hit, I *fumbled* the ball right to Todd.

BAM!

I didn't get knocked out, but by the time my eyes were able to focus again, Todd was being carried around the field.

Todd's dad stood over me.

"Are you all right?"

"Yeah, I think so."

With him not being the nicest dad in the world, it was surprising that he was concerned about how I was.

"Nice fumble, Little. You're just lucky Todd was there to pick it up."

Okay. That made a little more sense.

"Maybe next season you should try out for the girls' hockey team."

I see where Todd gets his sense of humor.

Milton stopped by to add his unwanted opinion.

"So, when it got to crunch time, the real Casey Little showed up. Pure one hundred percent chicken. Cock-a-doodle-doo."

"That was a rooster," I corrected.

"Yeah, right."

As he walked off, Nina came over to help me to my feet.

"That guy's a jerk," she said.

"Really?"

"You know, Case, if you didn't jump and get the ball, we would have lost."

"Thanks."

"I mean it. If I didn't know better, I'd think that you fumbled the ball to Todd on purpose."

"Yeah, right."

"I'm curious. Why aren't you using the Go-back to, you know, *fix* the end of the game?" she asked.

I looked over to where Mr. Dornan had his arm around Todd, telling anyone who cared to listen of Todd's heroic recovery of my "fumble." Todd cheerfully took it all in.

"Nah. I think I'll leave well enough alone."

"I don't get you, Case."

"Neither do I," I agreed.

"Well, if you're not going to do anything about it, I will," Nina said, pulling out the Go-back.

"Wait! Stop!"

"Hey. It stopped," said Nina.

She pushed the Go-back's button. But there was no SWOOSH. Not even a *swoo*.

"Did we go back?" she asked.

Just then Danielle yelled over to me. "Hey, Hands," she

said. "Maybe you shouldn't play another game until they start putting handles on footballs!"

"Does it look like we went back?"

She pushed it again.

"Now?" she asked.

I just smirked.

"Give me that," I said, taking it out of her hands.

The Go-back began to run again.

"It's working now," I said.

Nina grabbed it back. Just that fast, it stopped.

"No, it's not," she said.

And when I took it, it started once again. We did that back and forth about ten times. Every time Nina held it, it didn't work. Every time I held it, it did.

Now a lot of you might think that the reason it worked when I had it was because the Go-back was giving me the option; that it was allowing me to choose not only what would happen to me but how what I did affected others. Sort of choosing between right and wrong. It's a pretty complex idea. I mean, I have a hard enough time trying to figure out what's right or wrong for me. Like my life isn't tricky enough already.

Just then my dad came over.

"Don't worry, Case. You'll get 'em next time."

That felt good. Yep. This time I had made the right choice.

Not Bad.
Not Bad at All

Nina and I sat at Dom's eating pizza.

"So where's the Go-back?" asked Nina.

"I smashed it and threw it away," I said. "I decided that the rest of the world and I would be better off without it."

"Are you nuts? That could have been your ticket to success. If you didn't want it, you could have given it to me, you know."

"Like I said. The world's better off without it."

Howie, Jack, and Mel joined us.

"Why the gloomy puss, Nina?" asked Jack.

"Ah, nothing," Nina said pathetically. "Just watching time pass me by."

"This is just Nina's way of showing she's so happy that everything she ever does wrong will be one hundred percent her fault."

"Funny, Case," said Nina.

"What the heck are you guys talking about?" asked Howie.

Then, like clockwork, though not Go-back clockwork, Todd came over to badger us.

"I want to thank you, Little."

Wow. Did Todd have an idea of what really happened? Did he understand that circumstances are not always as simple as they seem? Did he know that I actually played some small part in his being the game's hero?

"Without you being such a total screwup, I wouldn't have had a chance to save the game."

I guess, in a way, he understood.

"I'm sorry to say that I'm going to have to take a pass on dunking you guys next week. My dad's taking me to Disneyland as a bonus for winning the game."

"We'll get by somehow," I assured him.

"Still trying to be a wise guy, huh?" asked Todd. "Maybe I'll just do a week's worth of dunking tonight."

As Todd went to grab me, he was pushed aside by the rubber-tipped end of a crutch.

"Excuse me," said Tractor. "Mind if I sit here?"

Everyone sat stunned. None of them had ever heard Tractor speak in public.

"Not a problem," I said.

Tractor slid in.

"Y'know, Todd. It's so nice of you to congratulate Little

for tapping the ball back to you after you screwed up and fumbled the ball away."

"Yeah," Todd said nervously. "But if I didn't—"

"And," Tractor added, "it's also nice that you're thanking him for lateraling the ball to you so you could score the winning TD."

"But that wasn't a latera—," Todd tried to say.

"And because you are going to thank him for that, I'm guessing there's no reason for you to be dunking him or anyone else anymore."

"Yeah. Well. Sure. Okay."

"Funny," said Tractor. "Maybe there's something wrong with my ears because I didn't hear you thank him yet."

Tractor shot Todd a big ole thirty-two-tooth smile.

"Well . . . ?"

Todd squirmed, then . . .

"Thank you for lateraling the ball to me so I could score the winning touchdown."

"I'm really sorry, Todd," said Tractor. "I don't think each one of those guys over at the counter heard you. And you probably want to say it with a smile on your face."

"Thank you, Casey," bellowed a grudgingly smiling Todd, "for lateraling the ball to me so I could score the winning touchdown."

"And this is just a guess on my part," added Tractor. "But I'm thinking you're not planning to try to stick my head in some toilet, are you?"

"No," said Todd. "Of course not."

"Well," said Tractor, "don't you think it would be a great idea if you stopped messing with everyone else?"

With the slightest of smirks, Todd shrugged.

"I'm sorry, Todd," I interjected, figuring I'd join in the fun. "I didn't hear that."

"I wouldn't push it," Tractor whispered in my ear.

"I won't be messing with anyone!" Todd blared as everyone at Dom's giggled.

"Good," said Tractor. "Look, I'm sure you want to get back to your pizza, but I want to thank you for being willing to share the credit for us winning the championship."

Todd, who seemed a bit smaller than when he first came over to the table, slumped back to his seat.

"Thanks," I said to Tractor.

"You know," said Tractor, "I'm not always going to be around, so starting tomorrow all of you losers are going to go through the Tractor Thinthith Toughening Up and Becoming Winners Camp."

"That's, um, really great," I said, not exactly looking forward to what was probably going to be a lot of work, but happy that I would no longer have to fear Todd. "Isn't there anything we can do in return?"

Tractor nodded ominously, then said, "Am I ever gonna get a chance to eat this pizza or do I have to dunk you guys in the toilet?" he growled.

After one uncertain beat, the table erupted in laughter. As we all continued to howl, I checked my pocket, making sure I still had the Go-back safely hidden and unsmashed. I may be a pretty good guy, but I'm not stupid.

As I stuffed my face, I couldn't help wondering if the Go-back knew how all this was going to work out. I didn't, but I did know one thing—this was going to be one heck of a ride.